I0768569

THE HARE IN HIS SNARE

JUNIPER HARTMANN

One of the biggest struggles I had writing this was the mention of protection. I figured it would be redundant to continue mentioning condoms and other preventative measures continuously, so I only did this once. I also didn't want to break the immersion in the fantasy... after all, isn't that half the fun of reading a book?

To that end, this novel mixes realism and fantasy. On one hand, I wanted it to be educational; on the other, I wanted it to be a really good time. I hope I was able to balance the two in a way that makes sense!

Just remember always to use protection when engaging in group dynamics. Safe sex is the sexiest kind, my friends.

Content Warnings

PLEASE READ

It is impossible to predict all triggers present in the audience. Please know that this is not a complete list of what may be upsetting.

If you find any of the following unacceptable, do not continue reading:

- *Dubcon / CNC*
- *Sharing / Group Sex*
- *Extreme BDSM*
- *Parent Loss*
- *General Trauma*
- *Mental Illness*

FOR ALL THOSE
WHO JUST WANT
SOMEBODY TO

LOVE THEM
EVEN WHEN
IT'S HARD

Chapter 1

She was late. She was never late. But it was ten minutes past the time class began, and she was late.

Bunny's black mules slipped across the linoleum as she rushed into the building, the heavy door swinging shut with a soft "whoosh" behind her.

There was a pounding between her ears, an echo of bad decisions ringing clear in the too-bright lights. Her eyes felt heavy in their sockets and her body screamed for hydration as she stumbled her way toward the lecture hall.

She reached her destination after another minute of traveling down one of the long, sterile hallways. Bunny took a deep breath, steeled herself for the looks, and opened one of the heavy double doors.

Heads swiveled from the long rows of white tables. Each face seemed surprised to see her. It was a large class, close to one hundred students, and the room was packed. While it was impossible to know every student, Bunny stood out due to her red hair and general reputation for punctuality.

If she was thankful for one thing, it was the coolness that brought relief to her feverish body as she slipped into the drafty auditorium. She pursed her lips and shuffled nervously to the front row. Her regular seat was dead-center… and taken.

Bunny took the next open option, bristling over the loss of her prime position. Almost as soon as she sat down, sliding her stack of notebooks from a leather messenger bag, she felt a looming presence.

Oh, for fuck's sake, She groaned internally, *Not this idiot.*

"Hey, there, Bunny," The upbeat attitude that poured from the TA always made her grind her teeth; it was easy to be happy when your head was empty.

"Hi," Her response was short and, she

hoped, conveyed her disinterest. As usual, Mark did not take the hint. He was infuriatingly good at ignoring her indifference to his advances.

"What held you up this morning? Normally you're quick as a bunny to class."

"None of your business, Mark. I have a headache. Go away," Bunny snapped, arranging her materials, and wincing inwardly. Mark wished her well and then walked back to the stage to wait for Professor McHardy.

With everything in order, Bunny crossed her arms and leaned back, surveying her surplus. There were colorful tabs, all coded to different types of information: statistics, quotes, important figures, and more. Her notebooks, each dedicated to the class name neatly written in block letters on their cover, were neatly organized and overflowing with information.

She would print out imagery and charts, taping them into the pages to ensure she had all of the details presented. She smiled to herself, thinking of McHardy, the doctor who would be center-stage soon. While he had a reputation for not taking things seriously, McHardy was taken seriously as an excellent source of valuable information regarding his field.

It had been during a sweltering, sweaty dig that she'd met the eccentric professor. Bunny had been assigned to his team for the excavation. It was part of an introduction to archeology class, a "fun" trip that would let the students get hands-on experience.

While she had bitched and moaned internally the entire time, Bunny found herself joyful as she lost herself to the process. There was something therapeutic about using the tiny tools to carefully extract remnants of the past.

She'd gritted her teeth and put up with bad puns and some jokes made in poor taste. Bunny had even sat with the man for lunch that day, sipping a cool drink and picking at a packed sandwich supplied by the college.

Her eyes had widened when he'd slipped a flask out of his jacket, holding his finger up to his lips and winking at her. At first, she had thought this was some ploy to get into her pants. Regardless, she'd accepted a hefty dose of liquor in her lemonade, and they'd spent the rest of the time in fierce discussion as the alcohol loosened their tongues.

Against her better judgment, Bunny began to like the man. This started his persistent but endearing campaign for her to transfer from pre-law into his department. She had originally taken the class for fun, and it did take some convincing, but Bunny eventually relented.

He had asked her, "Bunny, what's the point of being successful if you're unhappy? Go ahead, be a lawyer. Or you could come to learn about the things that actually bring you fulfillment and joy."

It was this piece of conversation that sealed the deal for her. What was the point of making herself miserable? She was already miserable enough most of the time. She didn't need to add to that.

McHardy finally sauntered in through his office door at the far end of the stage, waving a hand and apologizing for his tardiness. It was the same song and dance every time. While this happened, Bunny discreetly fingered through her bag, which she had hung on the corner of her chair, and pulled out a bottle with a label that stated "ibuprofen".

It wasn't ibuprofen.

She kept her anti-anxieties in the container to avoid advertising her access to a sought-after substance.

Popping a white disc into her mouth, she dry-swallowed it with what little spit she could conjure, desperately wishing she had something to drink. Pedialyte would be preferable, the electrolytes a balm on her pounding brain.

For a moment, the hairs on the back of her neck stood up, and she felt her skin shiver with rising goosebumps. Bunny turned her head and spotted Demetrius Ivanov staring at her. He was smiling softly in his self-assured way, but when his dark eyes met her blue-green gaze, they bored into her with an intensity that felt distinctly intimate. She looked away embarrassed, as though she were the one who had done something wrong.

The enigmatic man had been a thorn in her side for a few months now. She knew what he wanted, and she wasn't willing to give it to him. Demetrius Ivanov was not her cup of tea as a human being and she had no interest in what was between his legs. She wasn't going to be his flavor of the week.

Between Demetrius and Mark, she felt like screaming. This was her least favorite class, despite her favorite professor teaching it. She'd had plenty of interested men before, but never as acutely as Demetrius and Mark. She often wondered if it was some sort of competition, a pissing match between two men fighting for their mating rights.

Once McHardy had settled at the podium, he spoke into his microphone, leaning in a little too closely. "Is this thing on?" He guffawed at his own joke, unphased by the groans echoing through the room. He was tolerable because he was so jolly, even despite his corny humor. Bunny was ready for him to begin so she could lose herself in the lecture. With her nerves settling courtesy of a Benzo, she could relax into learning more about her chosen craft. Her heart always sang when she thought about her future career and working toward it.

Something about old things that brought peace to her. Even when she felt like falling in on herself, there existed proof that the crumbling evidence of humanity's accomplishments persisted even through abandonment and disuse. Maybe she could, too.

The class commenced and she dutifully transcribed everything on the board, drawing out and labeling diagrams and charts. Before she knew it, McHardy was winding down and going over the assignment due in the next class.

Bunny ensured she was out of the room and on her way home by the time his last sentence finished. Demetrius' advances had been growing insistent lately. With Mark as the TA in their shared class, he had been even more doggedly vying for her attention. Her desperation to avoid both of them was simply immeasurable.

Bunny could smell a playboy a mile away, and her nose wrinkled every time she got a whiff of Ivanov. She couldn't imagine flying through partners the way he did. It seemed cruel to play with a person's feelings, especially given the amount of girls on campus still pining for him.

The man was a predator in her eyes. Sure, his victims were willing, but he still ripped into their hearts with those perfect teeth all the same.

Once she was back in her dorm, Bunny unloaded her messenger bag from her shoulder and sank onto her plush bed, sighing when she felt the memory foam topper curve around her body like a hug. Her fingers played with the corner of her white duvet.

Fairy lights threaded through ivy hung above her bed, creating a beautiful twinkling effect through the plastic leaves. It shrouded her in shadows that shifted and slid over her body as the decorations moved under a softly blowing air conditioner.

She switched positions onto her back, throwing an arm over her forehead as she stared at the ceiling. It was a sparsely decorated space but one that she was proud to have. Bunny would never complain about having a safe place to lay her head at night.

After a few more minutes of resting, she decided it was time to start studying, but that thought quickly vanished as a knock sounded through the room. Hesitantly, she pushed herself off the bed and made her way over to the door. When she opened it, she had to bite back a groan. It was Michelle.

"Are you coming to the party tonight?" The blonde asked her, cocking her head slightly. She was already in a little red dress with matching boots. It was an adorable outfit that suited her small stature and full figure.

"What party?" Bunny asked, wary of the answer. There were plenty of places Bunny never wanted to visit again due to some unfortunate incidents that had happened her freshman year before she had learned to hold her liquor.

"That Ivanov dude who's into you is throwing down," Michelle responded excitedly. At that, Bunny blanched.

"Absolutely not."

"Bunny, don't be like that. Just come with us and enjoy the free alcohol. It's not like he's going to bother you with half of the graduate students there."

"You obviously don't realize how deep his obsession with me goes," Bunny responded dryly, fully aware that she would be their ticket into the party. Even if the house was full, Demetrius would always make an exception for Barbara Townsend.

Michelle wouldn't be ignored. This much she knew. And if she refused to accompany the group, she'd be on the receiving end of their ire for God knew how long.

"Okay, fine, whatever. I'm going to get ready," Bunny sighed, closing the door. She made her way to her wardrobe, looking through her options for the party. There wasn't much available in the way of choices. She was admittedly jealous of the girls who had closets stuffed full of club-ready clothing.

She, however, had a budget that forced her to choose between the business casual wardrobe she had carefully pieced together for class and internships, or having slutty dresses that made her feel like a queen. She couldn't afford to do both.

Finally, a white dress caught her eye. Bunny pulled it out and smiled, thinking of the way it would cling to her body. It was short, coming to her mid-thigh, and the material was silky soft. With a pair of elegant pumps, it could work.

Chapter 2

It was somewhere between summer and fall. The seasons were overlapping in a way that made the weather nearly impossible to predict. Having gambled and lost, Bunny was shivering as she wobbled slightly down the long gravel driveway toward the towering mansion that Demetrius Ivanov apparently called home.

She was unsteady in her red pumps, but not because of inability. In fact, Bunny often wore heels and had trained herself to walk in them properly. It was just so goddamn cold that her legs were shaking.

Her lips were painted the same bright red shade as her shoes. It was a vibrant color with blue undertones, making her pearly teeth pop. She had saved up money the previous summer to get them bleached. The cold was just another layer of misery she could add to her pile of complaints. Bunny wasn't here to enjoy the party, she was just here to help her friends out. Or, the people she hung out with. Bunny wasn't entirely sure she had real friends.

It was her own fault. She was forever busy studying or working, which left her falling through on plans. Her flakiness had earned her fewer invites as time stretched on until she had to be the one to approach others. The hard work would pay off, however. She had to work now to play later.

A couple of students stood at the towering double doors marking the entryway to the Ivanov household. They eyed Bunny and her friends as the group approached. Normally, they were there to check for IDs and turn away anybody underage.

"Hey, Bunny," One of them said as he opened one of the doors and the group of girls walked into the party. Inside, it was dark enough that the furniture appeared as faint shadows, outlines she could hardly make out. A faint neon glow guided the walkways, providing just enough light for the group to find a table full of liquor bottles. Demetrius was notorious for being a generous host, and girls always drank for free. They were more than allowed to help themselves.

Once they had cups full of more alcohol than mixer, they stood off to the side and took in the sights. They were in a cavernous room that Bunny assumed was supposed to be a family den when it wasn't filled with horny college students. People were grinding shamelessly against each other, mouths moving sloppily as they sought sexual gratification. Others milled about, drinking from red cups while they tried to find something, or somebody, to do.

Bunny scanned the room, a feeling of unease settling over her body, hair standing on end. She couldn't help but feel she was being watched again.

Then, she spotted him. He was standing on the landing at the top of the sweeping staircase. She could see better now that her eyes were adjusting to the low lighting. Beside him were what must be his close friends, but he stood apart from the group.

Demetrius was like a lion overlooking his pride, calmly satisfied with the results of his efforts. He was obviously on the hunt, however, based on the predatory gleam in his eyes as they landed on Bunny.

She shifted under the weight of his gaze, feeling like a prey animal who had wandered right into a trap; a snare had snatched her by the foot. Now, here she was, dangling in front of him like a dripping slab of meat. His gleaming teeth could rip and tear the flesh with ease if she let him.

Demetrius' friends were talking amongst themselves and didn't notice him walking away. Bunny, on the other hand, noticed this movement immediately. More importantly, she noted his trajectory. Her "fight or flight" instincts kicked in, and Bunny chose the latter. She turned and walked towards an open door behind her, unsure of where it led but not caring too much. Her friends didn't notice her slip away either, too caught up in a conversation with some men who had come to hit on them.

She wasn't certain she was allowed into this part of the house, and as she wandered down the hall, she realized that there didn't seem to be anybody else around anymore. Briefly, she felt bad, but a part of her was also certain he would securely close off anywhere he didn't want people going. Demetrius was a problem she had yet been unable to solve, but she couldn't deny that he was a thorough, observant person.

After all, she had been on the receiving end of his observational abilities regularly. It was strange to her, his obsession. She didn't understand how she had caught his eye in the first place— it wasn't as though he didn't have a string of women falling over themselves for him.

"Come out, come out, little Bunny…" When she heard his voice ring out, and the way he trailed off at the end with a laugh, Bunny felt her chest clench, shooting her heart into her throat. She couldn't see him and decided that it was best if he didn't end up seeing her, either.

What a creepy fucking dude… She thought to herself, surveying her options for evasion. There were a few different doors, and she was unsure where each one led. Bunny walked into one on her right, slipping in quietly. Looking around, she realized it was a bedroom. It was as dark as the rest of the house except for the peaceful streams of moonlight that soaked the room in a silvery glow.

"You know, this is a bit forward of you, Bunny."

She started at the sound of his voice.

Son of a bitch… she growled internally. Honestly, she wasn't sure why she thought he would fail to hunt her down. She turned, looking for an escape route, and found herself facing a gorgeous mirror. It was oval-shaped and had a thick, ornate golden frame.

"You're right. I agree that I am trying very hard to get you to understand that I don't like you," She spat back, "So, let me continue being forward as fuck." Her words were slightly slurred. The liquor she had consumed burned in her throat and she felt a little woozy. Distantly, she realized she was probably being more aggressive than usual.

To her surprise, he walked behind her, holding her hips and placing his neck over the curve of her shoulder so they were cheek-to-cheek. She could smell something like smoke and cedar wafting off of his warm body. Her eyes were locked on his arms around her waist in their reflection.

"See how good we look together, baby?" He murmured, squeezing his hands and earning a sharp breath from Bunny as she looked up into their faces. It was true. They would be a striking couple: her red hair even brighter next to the black of his. For a moment, she was caught in the pull of his gaze. His eyes were so intense it scared her. Bunny came to her senses and turned around, shoving him away from her.

"Not cool, Demetrius. I'm serious," Her eyes darted between him and the door he was blocking with his body. She wasn't in a mood to do this with him. He had never put his hands on her directly and Bunny decided she was not a fan. Demetrius followed her flicking eyes and seemed to pick up on her unease. He moved to the side, giving her a clear path out of the situation.

She didn't take it. Not quite yet.

"I don't get you, Bunny," He remarked, crossing his arms and cocking his head. Bunny felt like a lab rat, poked and prodded under his attention. It was as though Demetrius was actively trying to uncover whatever it was that made her tick. She didn't have time to respond because a new figure rushed into view.

"Demetrius, dude, look. We gotta talk," The newcomer was spitting his words out quickly, holding either side of the door frame as he leaned into the room.

"Who the fuck are you?" Bunny asked,

gesturing with a hand at the guy, exasperated with the turn of events.

He didn't even look at her, eyes trained on Demetrius even as he replied to Bunny, "Probably none of your fucking business."

"Michael, can you do me a favor and fuck off somewhere else?" Demetrius gritted out through his teeth, pinching his nose.

"C'mon, dude, I really need to talk to you," Michael whined, leaning forward.

"Let's walk through this together, Michael. Is this something you need to tell me right now? Is this something that can wait until tomorrow? And will receiving this information put me in a bad mood?"

"Yes, no, and no. It's about the coke and molly being here," Michael said back brightly, chuffed with himself for bringing the news. "Michael, I swear to God," Demetrius said evenly, "If you don't get out of this room, I will swing on you."

Taking his cue, Michael huffed, swung around, and walked away.

"You're telling me there are drugs in this house?" Bunny asked flatly as Michael disappeared. She sounded less than impressed with this news. Demetrius looked over at her, smiling sheepishly.

Before he could respond, she continued, "And I haven't been offered a single substance? Here I thought you were notorious for being such a generous host." She wasn't a stranger to party favors, especially when on a tight deadline and needing a little extra 'oomph' to get through.

Demetrius scoffed, "There's no way you're serious right now, Bunny. You've never touched a drug in your life."

"Assume harder, Demetrius. How do you think I make it through all of my finals?"

"Alright, fine. Follow me, then."

Chapter 3

Demetrius led her down the hallway and back into the din of the living room. They walked through another hallway, this one wider, and to a final door. Bunny shivered when she realized how secluded this part of the mansion was. If she screamed, would anybody even hear her? When he opened it, she noticed dark stairs descending into a pool of dim lighting.

"Uh," She said, suddenly unsure if this was a wise move, "Demetrius, where are you taking me?"

"The Chill Room, baby," He said, flashing a smile at her, "Relax. It's just the place we reserve for the most heinous of our debauchery."

"Wow. That's so reassuring," Bunny muttered. She was frowning but still decided to follow him as he started down the stairs, closing the door behind her out of habit. As she descended, she could see that the basement below was fully finished. There was a fireplace with plenty of comfortable seating arranged around it, as well as a large U-shaped couch surrounding a mounted TV on the other side. Bunny spotted people crowded around a table between the two points. Upon closer inspection, she realized they were doing lines.

The crowd noticed Demetrius and he was given a warm welcome. The men clasped his hand and slapped him on the back, grinning as their eyes flitted between him and Bunny. She shifted uncomfortably under their gaze; she was a rabbit in a wolf's den and the whole pack was home.

As if sensing her nerves, Demetrius demanded the room be cleared. There was little pushback from the rest of them as they shuffled out, obviously unhappy with their dismissal.

After they filed back upstairs dejectedly, Bunny looked at Demetrius, realizing they were alone together, tucked away in a sequestered place. She felt herself detaching from the situation, floating above her body as panic began to rise. What was she thinking? This was insanely dangerous.

His voice slammed her back to reality, "So, what's your pick of poison?"

"Usually weed, sometimes coke," She responded, crossing her arms and looking at the spread on the table. There were pills of every shade, shape, and size. Weed, of course, and some powders she wasn't sure she wanted to put a name to.

Demetrius hummed thoughtfully in response and picked up a grinder, opening it and pinching out a fair amount of finely ground green onto a rolling paper. She would guess he was putting down at least a couple of grams. The generosity didn't surprise her. He was likely hoping to get ass for grass.

It didn't take Demetrius long to roll. Bunny couldn't help but notice how good he was with his hands during the process. Once the joint was ready, he wet the paper with his tongue, and then rolled it in a white powder.

Bunny lifted an eyebrow. She'd previously had coke and weed together, but never when tipsy with a man she didn't know in a dark basement. Something just felt off about that, if she was being honest with herself.

Regardless of her reservations, Bunny found herself acquiescing to him as he motioned for her to follow. Demetrius walked around one of the long ends of the sectional, setting the ashtray on a coffee table that was nestled perfectly into the inner bend of the couch. She sat down next to him.

She didn't realize how sore her feet were until her weight was off of them. Bunny rolled her ankles slowly as she watched him light the joint, thinking back to the way his tongue gently slid across and flicked the paper.

Their history was short. Demetrius had approached her at a party a few months back and had been chasing her down ever since. He'd insisted that he wanted to take her out to dinner sometime, claiming to be enamored with her fierce intelligence. She had retorted that he could feel free to admit she was a nice piece of ass. When he had agreed, Bunny had told him to get fucked, and he had laughed like it was the funniest thing he had ever heard.

As she was unrelenting in her resistance, however, Bunny had proven herself a poor choice of prey. Nonetheless, Demetrius persisted. She knew very little about him, only that he was getting an MBA and lived at home with his parents just outside of town. Demetrius had always struck her as a bored playboy with too much family money.

Because of their difference in age and major, they hadn't had a single class together. She considered this a blessing. However, he had decided to take one of her classes this semester for no reason other than to be more persistent in his approach. It made the class miserable due to the other lost puppy pining for her affection.

Mark.

She looked over and noticed Demetrius was attempting to pass the joint, and they made brief eye contact. Bunny realized that they had been sitting in silence for a few moments, and she had been completely lost in thought.

"Anything you want to talk about?" Demetrius asked through the haze of smoke surrounding them in whirling grey wisps.

"No."

"That's okay."

Demetrius seemed amused, a little smile flitting across his lips before he pursed them to take another hit. Bunny caught herself staring at his mouth for a fraction longer than she should have and caught his gaze as she looked away.

His eyes were too knowing.

She blushed and cleared her throat, before saying, "I think I should get going."

"I think you should chill out for once, honey Bunny," He said softly, tone playful.

"What the fuck did you just call me?" Bunny whipped her head around to give him a look that conveyed her bewilderment. She continued, "No thanks on that, my guy. I'll pass."

Demetrius just chuckled in response, offering the joint once more. If he had planned to keep her longer, it seemed to be working, because she accepted it and took a long, crackling drag. Personally, she preferred blowing her lines, not smoking them. However, the delivery didn't matter as much as the high.

"I don't know. It just felt right. Probably because you're so sweet," His voice was higher and mocking in the second part of what he said.

"Okay, cool. Let's never have a repeat," She passed the stub of a joint back to him and stood up, the headrush making her dizzy, "Now, I'm actually going to go. But it's been great. Thanks for the drugs."

Demetrius also stood up, and she froze when she saw the glint in his eyes. Her throat tightened and a low fire lit up her belly. He offered to walk her out. She hardly heard him but agreed. They turned and started making their way around the couch. However, as they began walking toward the stairs, he grabbed her waist and gently leaned her toward the table.

"Hands on the table, Bunny," He purred in her ear. Bunny gasped and immediately complied. Once he began kicking her legs apart, she came back to her senses.

"What are you doing?" She yelped, turning around to push him away. Instead of moving back, Demetrius pulled her to his chest, steadying her wobbling legs. He smiled at her warmly before leaning forward.

"I want to make you feel good, baby. So, I'm going to," Demetrius murmured into her ear. The fire inside her roared and a pulse persisted between her legs even as she squeezed her thighs to dampen it. He turned her back around, and she put her hands on the table, briefly wondering what she was doing.

Demetrius pressed himself against her back, a hand coming around and lifting her dress to expose her white panties. He hooked a finger through the crotch of them, pulling them onto her thighs. Bunny gasped. Slipping between her labia, he quickly found her entrance and pushed two fingers inside of her, alternating between curling and thrusting.

She was surprised at how effective he was even with the awkward positioning.

"Already so wet for me, baby," He whispered, the other arm wrapping around her, pulling her closer so she could feel his hard cock pressing into her ass. Suddenly, she wanted it buried deep inside of her. Bunny knew she should resist, but she was horny.

So what if he was just looking for a conquest? She was just looking to get off.

Pulling his fingers from her, he traced up toward her clit and began toying with it. Bunny felt her hips buck and she let loose a noise she didn't realize she was capable of making. There was something about his expert touch that made her pleasure feel primal.

She panted and rocked her hips into his hands, too lost in a haze of colliding highs to say much of anything. Demetrius knew exactly what he was doing. Each little touch took her closer to the edge.

"I'm going to- I'm-" She stammered as she began falling over into oblivion.

And that's when he stopped.

Bunny whimpered and pushed her hips back into him, but he just moved out of the way as he withdrew his hand from between her legs after pulling her panties back up. She looked back, face red and eyes wide with shock, and realized at that moment that she was capable of murder. Demetrius stood there, licking a slick finger slowly while watching her impassively. He made no move to approach her.

"What are you doing?" She squealed, legs shaking from the horrible throbbing between them.

"I'm punishing you, Bunny. You can go home and fuck yourself all you want, but I promise nothing will compare to what I can do for you. I'll make you come when you've been a good girl and earned it."

Her heart hammered and her face burned bright. "Punishing me?" She spat out, "For fucking what?"

"For running from me earlier, when I had to follow you into the bedroom," With this,

Demetrius began walking to the stairs, "Don't ever make me chase you, Bunny, or you won't like what happens when I inevitably catch up."

She watched him in silence, absolutely dumbfounded by the entire ordeal.

"I'll let you recover, baby. You come back up when you're ready." With that, he flashed a dazzling smile and headed back upstairs.

Chapter 4

The cafeteria was the last place Bunny wanted to be. Between bright lights and the rich scent of breakfast, she felt like she was in hangover hell.

"Why do you let him call you 'baby'?" Michelle's question was fair, but Bunny wished her companion would stop talking. She hadn't been able to sleep until long after the sun came up, and then she was woken up for lunch only a couple of hours after finally dozing off. Bunny was nursing a pounding headache that Michelle's incessant babbling did nothing to help. Her stomach was barely holding on.

"Because he won't stop," She groaned, folding her arms on the table and putting her head down.

"What do you mean?" Michelle asked, oblivious to Bunny's discomfort.

"It doesn't matter how many times I've told him to fuck off. He just keeps doing it," Bunny ground out, hoping it would be the end of the conversation. Luckily for her, Michelle had to rush off to class, and she left.

After the painkillers she had taken had kicked in, she decided to read. The sun shone through the floor-to-ceiling windows next to her table, bathing her in a warm, golden glow. Even if she had woken up hungover after the biggest mistake of her romantic life, she could still make it a good day. She did just that for a good stretch of time before he arrived. Smoke and cedar filled the air around her and Bunny immediately felt herself cringe.

"Well, if it isn't Miss Honey Bunny herself," Demetrius said, grinning like a fool. *No, not 'like a fool,'* She thought to herself, *He is a goddamn fool.* She heaved a mighty sigh before setting down the book she had been buried in. It was an incredible read and she was more than a touch grumpy that she'd been interrupted.

He swung into the seat across from her. The table was only big enough for two, so he took up almost the entire surface area when he leaned forward.

"How do you like your tea?" Demetrius asked, as he picked the cup up and took a sip.

"Hey, excuse me!" She exclaimed, mouth gaping, "Are you serious?"

"That's pretty good. Needs more milk and sugar, though."

"What the fuck, Demetrius?"

He only held her gaze in response before saying, "So, when do I see you again?"

Bunny leaned back, arms crossed, feeling distinctly unamused by him.

"You're looking at me right now."

"You know what I mean."

"Why would I want somebody who looks like their only personality trait is liking Franz Ferdinand looking at me?"

He looked genuinely wounded, "Franz Ferdinand was a very important historical figure."

"Wrong Franz Ferdinand, Demetrius. Also, not the point."

"Exactly my point, Bunny. Let's stop dancing around the real topic, which is when you come to my house and show me all of the music out there that's apparently better than Franz Ferdinand. Should I pick you up tonight, or…?"

"No."

"What do you mean 'no'?"

"I mean what happened was a mistake that I will not be making again. It was fun, and now it's over."

Demetrius smiled wider and wider as she spoke, eyes gleaming with something that made her squeeze her thighs together. He didn't respond at first, just held her gaze as she uncomfortably recollected the way he'd bent her over a table just the previous night.

She broke first and looked away.

"You know what I think, Bunny?" He whispered, leaning forward with his gleaming teeth bared in a curling grin, "I think you went home last night and you touched yourself for hours trying to recreate what I made you feel," He wet his lips before continuing, "And I bet you couldn't even come close."

Bunny recoiled internally. Not because he was wrong, but because he was right. With that, Demetrius stood up and walked away.

In a rush once again, Bunny bumped into an obstacle in her path and looked up with a gasp. Technically, it was a person, and she wasn't sure if people counted as obstacles.

Until she saw who it was.

Mark stood there, passive and happy as usual.

Alright, definitely an obstacle, she thought. Bunny gritted her teeth into a makeshift smile and briefly offered her apologies. Before she could walk around him into class, he reached out and grabbed her elbow, "Bunny, wait."

She turned her head to look at him and caught Demetrius' gaze while doing so. He was locked onto the situation like a hawk. Sensing an opportunity, Bunny turned fully. She reached out, lightly pressing her hand against his shoulder.

"I'm so sorry, Mark, I just wasn't watching where I was going," She whined, pouting a little at the end.

"You're totally fine. Don't even worry about it," He responded, perking up at her unusually positive response to his attention.

"No, really, I should have been looking where I was going," She let her hand fall from his shoulder to his chest, "Maybe I can make it up to you sometime?"

Mark stammered out his agreement and they arranged the details quickly, taking out their phones to text each other. Bunny could have sworn he'd drop dead when she handed over her number.

When she glanced over her shoulder, Demetrius was all but boiling over the edge. His eyes met hers briefly, but they stayed on Mark for the rest of the class. She didn't want Demetrius to hurt him, but she did want to send a clear signal that she was still very much single.

She was *not* his girl.

———

Unfortunately, Demetrius did manage to catch her after class. He'd simply brushed his hand against her hip as he walked by. She'd stiffened but hadn't reacted further. Bunny wasn't about to give him the satisfaction. Her phone rang and she pulled it out of her bag, brightening at the name.

"Hey, Brianna," She said, "How are things?"

"They're great, Bunny! Really great. Hey,

I think I have the perfect import for you. Already stateside and in our area! I'm sending the details over. Let me know when you can come do stalls tomorrow, and I gotta go."

"Sounds good! Probably like seven. Bye!"

The call ended abruptly and Bunny was still grinning as she opened her messages. Promptly, that smile was wiped away. The name of the owner glared at her from the screen: Katarina Ivanov.

Ivanov… No fucking way, She thought to herself, *Right?* She had been trying to purchase a horse for a few months now, looking high and low for a specific animal that would help her move up the levels without moving her back into poverty.

Brianna had been her instructor and friend for many years, so she was overseeing the shopping process. She had become family over the years and often acted as a mother figure once she realized Bunny was severely lacking in that area. Ever strong-willed and sure of herself, Bunny admired the woman's intensity.

The name on the papers wouldn't deter her. If Brianna sent her a horse, it was for a damn good reason. Besides, there was no way there was any relation between Demetrius and the owner.

It had to be a coincidence.

Chapter 5

It was not a coincidence.

As it turned out, Katarina was his mother, and Demetrius was the only person able to show her the horse. Katarina had reiterated in a thick Eastern European accent that her boy knew his way around a barn and would be a suitable stand-in. Bunny didn't have the heart to tell the woman that she already knew her son, and didn't like him very much at all.

She knew that this was a mistake before she even pulled up to his house. Her reliable little Subaru shone brightly blue in the sunlight. It was a gorgeous day, a cool breeze bringing the first traces of Autumn to the air. Before heading to his family's estate, she had thought to stop at a car wash. She was sure she would seem unpolished enough to these people as it was. It only occurred to her afterward that it was a waste of time since his parents were gone and she certainly wasn't trying to impress him.

Bunny stepped out onto the gravel. It was a large circular driveway with a fountain in the middle featuring two rearing horses. While the previous party had brought her to his doorstep, it had been dark and she hadn't gotten a chance to really look around. It was absolutely gorgeous. The architecture impressed her, with sweeping arches and towering windows.

Looking over after hearing footsteps on the gravel, she watched Demetrius making his way toward her. His hand shielded his eyes from the sunlight. Apparently, the idiot hadn't even thought to wear sunglasses. Bunny had.

"Hey, Bunny, we're going to start in the kitchen," His grin was dazzling, white rows of perfectly straight teeth shining in the sunlight.

She grabbed her riding helmet and tall boots from the backseat of her car as he spoke, already wearing a polo and breeches. Bunny turned to face him as she rolled her eyes dramatically.

"Demetrius, this isn't a social call. I'm

here to try a horse. That's it."

"Correct. However, I've been working my ass off in the barn all morning to prepare for exactly that. I need something to ingest before I pass out."

Without another word, he turned. Bunny marched behind him, looking around once again. She had hardly seen a more grand place. *What do his parents do for work? And how do I do it, too?* She thought bitterly to herself.

They walked in through the set of towering double doors at the front entrance. Bunny could hardly contain the gasp that almost left her mouth once she saw the space in the light for the first time.

There was an elegant chandelier hanging above. It was an open-concept room with a large staircase leading to the upstairs, with no ceiling separating the two floors. There was also what looked like a screened-in porch to her right that she hadn't noticed from the outside, but she only caught a glimpse through the door as she followed Demetrius through one of the hallways.

He led her down to a room at the end, which opened up to a kitchen she'd kill for. The black cabinetry had gorgeous dark oak finishes, the same found throughout the rest of the furnishings. It was a combination that left her spellbound. Demetrius didn't seem to notice.

Instead, he walked to the counter and rummaged through a cabinet until he pulled out a blender. She assumed he was making a protein shake. When he took out a bottle of tequila, she huffed.

"I thought you said you needed something to eat?" Her voice was dripping with agitation.

"No, I didn't. I said that I needed to ingest something. It just so happens that the 'something' is a margarita."

He walked over to the fridge for mixer and a lime. Once he had the supplies, he deposited them onto the counter. Demetrius then took the blender and filled it with ice from the dispenser.

Bunny had never had a refrigerator that dispensed ice until she moved into her dorms.

"I'd offer you one, but I'm not entirely certain your alcohol tolerance is very high after last time I saw you drunk. You're a little sloppy, honey Bun'," He smiled wickedly at her. His words were a barb, even as she knew they rang true. Her tolerance wasn't very good. He had seen proof of that with their previous encounter.

Still, she bristled at the dig and proceeded to snap back, "Yeah, because you were so put together. I'll actually take one if you don't mind. I think I'm going to need it."

Demetrius glanced at her, an eyebrow raised, before turning back to dump an orange base into the blender. Within a minute, he was pouring them both a glass in large mason jars.

"Obnoxious choice of drinkware. I didn't take you for a hipster," Bunny said as she took hers, "What flavor is this, anyway?"

"Mango," He responded, looking over his glass at her, and taking a sip immediately after.

Bunny loved mango. She drank a bit herself and was pleasantly surprised that Demetrius knew how to make a drink to her taste. She hadn't breathed a word of her preferences to him, so it must have been how he preferred them, as well.

It wasn't strong, just enough so that she could taste traces of the tequila in the sweet slush. She begrudgingly realized that this also reflected well on Demetrius; he wasn't trying to get her wasted by spiking it with a ton of alcohol. She had been worried about that, especially since they were alone.

He moved towards a door with a frosted glass pane that had sunlight streaming through it onto the rich oak flooring, wincing as the door opened. She put her sunglasses back on because she wasn't an idiot. It then struck her as odd that he had such a reaction to bright light.

"You know, dark eyes have high levels of melanin, Demetrius," She mused, "Which means you wincing every time you go outside makes you look like a little bitch."

"You know what I've always liked about you, Bunny?" He asked without missing a beat, apparently unphased, "I love that you're just so sweet."

She made a noise of acknowledgment, a little miffed that she hadn't struck his ire. Bunny had been trying to do the opposite of win him over for ages now. Foolishly, she had first believed being rude to him would fend him off. Instead, he seemed to either not care about her digs or, worse yet, found them entertaining.

The door opened up to a cobblestone path through a gorgeous garden, with a small fountain and seating to the right. Flowers bloomed in full, covering the space to either side of the walkway in a bright swath of color. Towering sunflowers lined up to the edge, hovering over them as they continued toward a black-painted brick arch covered in hanging ivy. Bunny took it all in. The air was thickly perfumed with a rich scent she sucked in greedily. Realizing she was sniffing at the air, she felt her face flush. Demetrius threw a look over his shoulder, eyes crinkling good-naturedly, She knew he was smiling.

A fan of my father's garden?" He questioned, looking ahead again as they walked through the arch.

"Sure. It's fine," Bunny responded dismissively.

The rest of the walk to the barn she could see over a hill was quiet but, to her dismay, enjoyable. Bunny felt a sense of peace and awe in her surroundings. There was a twang of jealousy, but she had been around wealth enough due to her work with horses to stop feeling as envious as she once had.

They walked into the aisle of an impressive but understated barn. The white double doors were pulled back and a rubber rope ran across the entrance, meant to keep loose horses from running out.

Demetrius unclipped it and motioned for

her to walk through. She did so stiffly but then stopped in her tracks to marvel at the interior. There was another chandelier, this one smaller and between a series of decorative rafters that lined the ceiling.

The architecture was gorgeous, a combination of black steel and dark oak paneling. It was relatively small, with only six stalls, but each one housed a stunning animal. There were bars instead of walls, which was something she loved. It allowed the horses to see each other, which kept stress levels to a minimum. Bunny was melting as her eyes passed from one area to the next.

"Go ahead and say hi," Demetrius said, clipping the rope back in place, "They're all friendly. Even the stallions."

She walked up to the first stall on her left and read the golden nameplate, which was engraved with the name, "Maximum Overdrive." She could tell immediately he was a stallion from his heavy huffing on her hand, which she held out before placing it on his nose just below his eyes.

"Hello, beautiful," She whispered, stroking his snout while bringing up her other hand to pat his neck. The horse went to swing his head forward and she gripped the bone in his nose. Bunny pushed firmly down to stop him from ramming his head into her face.

"We're still working on his manners," Demetrius called from the other end of the aisle, likely retrieving the horse she was here to look at. Finally, they were getting to the point she had been itching for during her entire time with him.

But now, with these extravagant horses surrounding her, she didn't want the moment to end. She wanted to go from stall to stall, looking over everything this place had to offer.

Bunny would have gladly traded her soul for this exact setup. It was her dream, made solid in front of her. She felt the stirrings of resentment again deep in her chest and did her best to stifle them. In the same way that her life wasn't her choice, neither did Demetrius have the option to pick his own.

A gorgeous gelding was led from the stall Demetrius was in, the tall horse shining under the overlights. He was a beautiful shade of bright chestnut, with three socks and a stocking.

Demetrius noticed her looking at the markings, raising his eyebrows, and asking, "Big fan of chrome?" He was referring to the white markings.

"Yeah, you could say that," She responded.

Bunny walked over as he clipped the animal into cross-ties and began readying him for a ride. When Demetrius started chatting to her, she gave one-word responses. As the margarita began to disappear, however, her tongue loosened and she moved on to sentences.

"Why don't I go refill our glasses and you can finish tacking up?" He said. She agreed and finished the process. When he returned, they walked out of the barn and into the arena, where they continued talking about a variety of topics as the conversation shifted comfortably from one point to the next.

It was lovely, and Bunny *hated* it.

Chapter 6

She was sitting on his bed, holding a joint to her lips, a third margarita sitting empty on the bedside table. If you had told her this is where the day would end up, Bunny would have told you to put the crack pipe down. Demetrius was leaning against the headboard beside her, too close but not enough for her to complain. She just didn't like being crowded.

"So, why archeology?" He asked, taking the joint back from her between two pinched fingers.

"Because I like things old," She said, laughing a little as she answered, "Especially my men."

"I didn't realize digging for gold was part of the curriculum for your major. You go,

Yosemite Sam," Demetrius choked out around a smoky exhale.

She smacked his arm.

What she had said was clearly directed at him, another hole she tried to poke in his plans to pursue her. She still felt his longing gaze lingering a little too much now and again. It made her distinctly uncomfortable, but not in an unpleasant way. No, Bunny was simply upset with the way her heart beat a little faster and her blood ran a little hotter when she could smell him in the air.

She stood up suddenly and Demetrius started, head whipping to look at her, mouth ajar. Whirls of smoke lifted from the end of the joint.

"What are you doing?"

"I think it's time I got going. I've been here a while and I have some tests to study for and I have to be at the barn at six in the morning tomorrow," She was rambling at this point, flushed and desperate to see herself out before she did anything she might regret.

Demetrius stood up, putting the joint out on an ashtray. The four-poster bed was pushed up against a wall with bay windows to either side of it. It was impeccably outfitted with elegant furnishings that made it look more like a study than a bedroom. There were towering bookcases built into one wall, while another boasted a seating area in front of a fireplace.

He reached out for her wrist and the contact sent shivers up her quickly slackening spine.

"Wait," He said, sounding desperate.

"No, Demetrius, I have to go," She insisted, pulling her wrist out of his loose grip.

Without further warning, Demetrius lunged forward and used his body to press Bunny into a small space of wall between the bed and window. She gasped, her hands thrown up to rest gently against his chest. It was originally a motion to push him away, but she realized that she didn't want to.

Instead, when he pressed his lips to hers, she softened into their tender push. Bunny sighed as he pulled away, her eyes closed to slits. She was lost in a haze of weed, alcohol, and lust.

At her sigh, Demetrius moved a hand between their bodies and cupped one of her breasts. Bunny pressed into his touch, whimpering slightly as her face flushed. His other hand was gripping her hips, while his mouth moved once more in sync with her swollen lips.

At what he took as a positive signal, Demetrius slowly slipped a hand up her shirt, ran his fingers under her bra, and held the warm mound of her breast in his hand. Bunny rolled her back forward and he chuckled into her mouth. She was absolutely ravenous for him.

When he put a hand down to grab her knee, hitching her leg over his hip, Bunny allowed the movement without hesitation. She then ground her core against his hip, mewling into his mouth as his hand began working a nipple, tight with need.

"Just like that, Bunny," Demetrius panted, "We both need this, baby."

He moved both hands under her ass and lifted, Bunny's legs wrapping around his waist. Once he had brought them to the bed, he laid her down gently, pressing her into the comforter with his body. Their lips hadn't parted since he spoke and Bunny's hands were now cupping Demetrius' face, evidence of a gentleness in her that she hadn't thought he'd experience with her.

"I need to go get a condom. You're going to play with that pretty pussy while I do that." He had pulled away, earning a sound of indignation from her. Bunny sucked in sharply and then said, "Excuse me?"

She couldn't hide the waver in her voice that likely betrayed her quickly building desire, even as her first instinct was to reject the order on principle. In response, she felt Demetrius gently grasp her hand and migrate it down to her still-clothed core. He unbuttoned her pants and then slid her hand down until her fingers were just at the edge of her panties.

"I want to watch you touch yourself, Bunny. So, you're going to work your clit until I'm satisfied."

Bunny's cheeks and belly were both burning. Her heart had quickened and she could feel herself panting lightly. She didn't want to comply with him just as badly as she did. As if in a trance, never breaking contact with his deep, cool gaze, Bunny dipped her fingers deeper until she reached her labia.

She was already slick with desire.

Dragging her wetness upward, she began circling that little bud that burned for attention. Her lips parted further and her eyes widened at the shock that shot through her as soon as she touched her swollen clit.

"That's my good girl. Just so we're clear, Bunny, this ends whenever you want it to. Say the word and it all stops."

But his voice was distant as her head fell back and she unashamedly twirled her fingers, working herself without pause. The sensations made her body pulsate with pleasure. She could feel his eyes on her, and knowing she was being watched only seemed to intensify the experience. She was so *exposed*.

Bunny continued whimpering; she couldn't help herself. It was the type of sensation that made her choke on her own breath as she let go of everything except the overwhelming feelings exploding from between her legs.

Chapter 7

When Demetrius returned, he threw a condom on the bed and then leaned down to kiss her. Once he pulled away, he pulled her off the bed. Bunny stood on uneasy legs, the pleasant buzz making the floor below her feet feel unsteady.

But it wasn't the alcohol driving her actions; the issue was that her body couldn't be ignored. She was clearly receptive to Demetrius' advances. And here she was, following along like a puppy on a leash while a man led her through the motions once again.

She watched as he knelt, peeling her breeches down her legs, holding her steady as she stepped out of them. He came back up and Bunny shivered under the slow slide of his hands up her body as he lifted her shirt off her head. Bunny stood there in her bra and panties, feeling wildly vulnerable. She crossed her arms in front of her chest, hunching in on herself.

Demetrius gently gripped her forearms and pulled her arms back to her sides. "No, Bunny. I won't let you hide from me. But if you want this to end, it will. Immediately. I don't want you to do anything you don't want to."

Pulling her bottom lip between her teeth, Bunny felt a flush creep across her cheeks. She glanced up only once at his gaze, intense and unflinching. He seemed entirely impassive. It felt as though he was treating her like a frightened animal, staying calm and moving slowly.

The thought made her feel simultaneously opened up and closed off. She didn't want him to see her like this. What am I doing? She thought to herself, someplace inside her mind still railing against what her body cried out for.

"I want this, Demetrius. I do," She admitted in a breathy whisper.

He guided her back onto the bed, this time directing her onto her hands and knees. Bunny shivered in anticipation as he hooked a finger through her panties and pulled them from her body in one smooth motion. She loved being pounded with her face buried in a pillow.

But he didn't kneel behind her. Instead, he laid on his back with his head between her knees. Bunny looked down and locked her gaze with Demetrius as he pulled her hips down toward his face with one hand while the other came up to press the small of her back, the arched position placing her core directly in front of his face. Bunny watched in awe as he ran his tongue over her outer lips, and then parted them right outside of her opening.

He licked up towards her clit. Bunny whipped her head back and cried out once he began using his mouth to make her feel things she didn't think were possible.

Struggling to sit up, she fell forward and planted her forearms on the bed to steady herself. Demetrius grabbed her hips to keep her pussy flush with his face and then ground her against himself. She followed the movement immediately, whimpering and crying out. He reached one hand up to tweak one of Bunny's tender nipples.

She was desperate at this point, bucking and writhing with pleasure. Her breasts had always been so sensitive, responsive to even a feather-light touch. Demetrius switched between pinching gently, rubbing a thumb around it, and tweaking it. It was a delicious, heady mixture that made her feel wild with need.

She was so close to her climax. Her pussy pulsed as her walls began fluttering, and her cries became more animalistic…

And then Demetrius stopped, lifted her hips, and slipped out from under her. Bunny choked out a gasp, turning her head to look at him with wide, yearning eyes.

He looked pleased with himself now, and he crawled around her so that they were level. Demetrius cupped her cheek before saying, "You were such a good girl for me. I love how you taste, baby."

Bunny closed her eyes and gulped, a fire building in her torso. His words shivered through her body. She was desperate for more even while her mind still insisted this was a terrible idea and could only end badly. She had heard the stories. She knew that he would discard her promptly once he was finished.

He had finally won his prize. But right now, she didn't care.

Demetrius pressed his lips into hers and

they stayed locked in a deep kiss. She could taste the evidence of her pleasure on his tongue. It was faintly sour, but not unpleasantly so, with just a trace of vinegar. She moaned deeply.

He broke away and took her bra off before helping her to lay on her back. Demetrius then lay between her legs, still completely clothed. She wondered briefly when he planned on taking off what he was wearing.

Once he was holding himself above her with his elbows, Demetrius cupped her face in both hands. He leaned down to press a light kiss on her forehead. Dark, sultry eyes stared into hers and she could feel her heart pick up speed. It skipped beats in a way she had never felt before.

"Are you sure you want this, Bunny? Do you want my cock?" He murmured.
Bunny closed her eyes and wet her lips before responding, "Yes."

"Then be a good girl and ask me nicely."

"I really want this, Demetrius, I swear."

"I don't think you understand, Bunny," He leaned in closer to her, "I want you to say, 'Please, I want your cock.'"

She could smell herself mixed with tequila and weed on his breath. Sucking in through her nose and staring incredulously at him, Bunny felt her heart thump at the command. He couldn't be serious. Giving into him by itself was already thoroughly humiliating and she could feel that familiar burn in her face.

And yet, she found herself quoting him verbatim. She looked up at him through her lashes submissively as she spoke, "Please, I want your cock."

In response, Demetrius sat up and began taking his clothing off. She admired his physique; muscular, but lean. He rippled with enough muscle so that she knew he must lift weights, but not so much that he bulged.

Except for one place.

Bunny gulped at the evidence of his arousal. From what she could see, his rock-hard cock was sizable. She hadn't taken anything on the larger side of the scale. Really, she hadn't had very many partners at all. She just didn't have the time for romance.

Out of the small pool, none of them had been so attentive as Demetrius had so far. Bunny breathed a little harder remembering the feeling of his tongue in places that had never experienced that treatment. Not a single person had ever eaten her out. She had no idea it would be that good.

I can't ever tell him that, She thought, *He'll be such a smug asshole about it.*

Demetrius slipped on the condom and then laid between her legs again. She was correct: his veiny manhood stretched on for what felt like far too long, the girth giving her pause as he positioned himself.

He lowered his body so he was lightly pressed into her. Demetrius whispered, "Are you ready, baby?" She had spread her knees, leaning them towards the bed to widen his access.

"Please, I want it so bad," Bunny mewled before she could stop herself. She didn't think she could take it if he decided to stop at this moment. No amount of masturbation could possibly replicate the pleasure he was granting her.

Demetrius shifted his hips forward, gently pushing inside of her. She whimpered and wiggled her hips, encouraging him deeper. He complied.

Bunny released a throaty moan into the space between his collarbones, pressing her lips to his skin once she was done crying out. He began thrusting and, little by little, buried himself inside of her. Bunny wrapped her legs around his hips and shifted, feeling his entire length inside of her.

It was almost uncomfortable, on the edge of painful, but not quite over it.

Demetrius ducked his head so that he could capture her lips again. Again and again, he expertly guided his hips in and out of her, fanning the inferno rapidly building in her belly. She was so close to her orgasm, just from penetration.

"Ask before you come, baby," He whispered in her ear after he broke their kiss.

"W-what?" She whined, rolling her hips to meet his as he ground into her.

"I want you to ask my permission before you come," His voice was soft as silk but had a hard edge to it, even as he was huffing through the sentence. Bunny gasped as he punctuated each word with a slam of his hips. She buried her head back into his chest. The very thought made her want to backhand him.

As she waged an internal war, Bunny suddenly felt herself toppling over the edge. Her entire body tensed, back arching and mouth widening. She was wailing as the release sent shockwaves rippling through her body.

Demetrius stopped thrusting, and she let out a yelp at the sudden lack of stimulation.

"You're not very good at following directions, are you, Bunny?" He murmured in her ear, stroking her cheek with the back of a finger on the other side of her face.

"Excuse me?" She stammered out, still burning with the need for more.

"I think somebody deserves to go over my knee for not listening."

Bunny's eyes widened and her heart went off the rails. *He wants to… Oh, oh,* She thought, short-circuiting as the sultry imagery played in her mind. The idea of being punished like an insolent brat made her squirm almost as much as the sheer humiliation of being put over his knee and spanked.

"I-" She started, then abruptly stopped as he spoke again,

"This only goes as far as you want it to, honey Bunny. If you're uncomfortable at any point, we can stop. How about you say the word, 'fire hydrant' to signal to me?"

Bunny swallowed hard and then murmured her agreement. "I want it," She whimpered, "I want it so badly."

And she did. She was desperate to feel the sting of shame, embarrassment, and pain. He rolled off of her and sat on the edge of the bed, pulling Bunny over to him and draping her over his lap. She panted, face on fire and hands gripping the sheets.

Demetrius rubbed her ass with his hand, using the other hand to reach over and cup her chin. He gently asked, "Are you sure, baby? Do you really want this? Do you remember your safeword?"

Bunny whimpered, "Please, I need it. Yes. Fire hydrant. Please."

She released a pained yelp as he hit her for the first time. This was followed by a series of hard smacks until her face was buried in the sheets as a sharp throbbing developed. Bunny could feel tears pricking at her eyes as a series of intense emotions ripped through her.

Wriggling and whimpering, she finally screamed, "Fire hydrant," feeling briefly silly.

Demetrius immediately stopped and rolled her over, pulling her to his chest, "Are you okay, Bunny?" He purred, gently stroking her cheek.

Bunny pushed away from him immediately, standing on wobbling legs as her head spun with the rush of the past hour.

"I shouldn't be- this isn't-" She kept stammering, shaking slightly as she backed away from him. Demetrius stood, eyes alert and attention fully on her. She froze as he approached, staying still even as he pulled her to his chest.

Then Bunny burst into tears.

Demetrius took her to the floor, settling her across his lap and wrapping his arms around her so that she was surrounded by his embrace.

"Shhh, baby, I know. It was intense," He whispered, rocking her gently as he peppered her face with soft kisses. The gentle treatment only made her sob harder into his chest.

"I'm s- sorry," She choked out, "I'm so sorry," She felt intensely shameful that they had fucked and she became a sloppy bitch afterward. Bunny had never cried after sex. But Demetrius was so calm and gentle that she felt safe for the first time in losing herself to the horrible sadness that always loomed. Her thoughts raced with a multitude of memories; flashes of abuse, and emotions lingering from neglect she had faced.

And here was Demetrius, holding her the same way she had always wished somebody would have.

He waited for her sobs to subside to sniffles before speaking. "Let's get you cleaned up, Bunny."

Before she could protest, he stood, lifting her with him. It felt like he didn't expend any effort at all to do so, and Bunny only felt more fragile for it. He walked her to the door at the other end of the room, opening it with one hand and walking her into a gorgeous bathroom.

Once they were settled, Demetrius sat at the edge of the garden tub, holding her close to his chest. She settled in his lap as he leaned forward to turn on the faucet, then plugged the drain. She didn't say anything, hiding her face in his chest.

"You're okay, baby, I promise," Demetrius murmured into her ear, "I'm here. I know." She couldn't even argue with him. Something inside of her, some piece she wasn't even aware was broken, rubbed its jagged edges against her organs. It seemed to pierce her everywhere all at once.

He turned the tap off and slid her into the water. She resisted letting go of him at first, but the tub was just so inviting. The water surrounded her like an embrace and she let herself sink until just her face was above the surface.

Once she was settled, he stepped into the tub, standing behind her. Demetrius crouched down carefully and then sat so that the top of her forehead brushed against his stomach, his legs stretched in front of him. He grasped her hips and pulled them so that her head slid up and she was sitting between his legs. Demetrius pulled her to his chest and kissed her neck.

Bunny whimpered in response, letting her head roll back to rest on his shoulder. She could feel his cock harden again underneath her and feared he would want to take her again. She wasn't in a position to stop him, but she also didn't want it.

He surprised her, however. Instead of making a move to initiate more sex, he began pouring soap into a washcloth. Demetrius hugged her to his chest with one arm and began gently cleaning her with the other.

While he did this, she relaxed into him. Bunny wrapped her arms around his bicep, resting her head in that dip between his shoulder and neck. He still smelled so good. It was more than just smoke and cedar. Now, she could smell his sweat and her arousal that still sat on his tongue as he spoke.

"You did so well for me," He whispered into her hair as he rubbed her back with the cloth, "I loved hearing you scream while I worshiped your body."

Bunny was on another plane of existence. The entire day had been a rollercoaster, and she felt like she was going to pass out. From showing up, and sipping margaritas while chatting pleasantly with him, to the crush of their bodies, to his hand against her ass, to this… She was exhausted.

Once he was done, he stood, gently pulling her up to stand. She was still clinging to his bicep. Bunny snuggled into his body with a sigh. She was content to lean against him and allow Demetrius to move her about as necessary.

He turned on the spray and cleaned the suds from their naked bodies. Once he had thoroughly ensured they were clear, especially between her legs, Demetrius stepped out of the tub and helped Bunny do the same. She wobbled out and allowed him to wrap her in a towel.

Demetrius led her out of the bathroom

by taking her hand and gently pulling her along. Once in the bedroom, he helped towel her off and slipped one of his t-shirts over her head. She swam in it.

From there, she was escorted to his bed and he pulled her into his arms. They were facing each other, and he had pulled her into a tight hug. Her face rested against his chest and she was lured to sleep, but not before she heard his soft voice.

"You were such a good girl for me tonight, Bunny." He was stroking her hair softly. Her ass still smarted from her time over his knee, but it was a pleasant throb.

Demetrius kissed the top of her head. They both slept, clinging to the other for comfort.

Chapter 8

Bunny woke up to gentle kissing on her neck. Her eyes fluttered, confusion blooming as she came around. Reality hit her like a ton of bricks. Her first thought was that she had fucked Demetrius Ivanov. The second was that he hadn't even gotten off, which seemed odd.

She moaned in surprise when she felt teeth sink softly into her shoulder. His efforts to wake her were paying off, but Bunny was ready for war. She could feel the weight of a hangover overhead and knew she would be waking up to a nightmare, and not just due to headaches and nausea.

"Good morning, good morning," The sing-song voice made her groan, and she shoved him weakly as he wrapped his arms around her waist and pulled her close to him.

"Fuck off," She said, burying her face in the pillow.

"Face out of the pillow, Bunny. I'm the only one allowed to bury your face in a pillow like that."

Her head shot up, and she fixed a venomous glare on him, only to realize she had done exactly as he had told her to.

"Breakfast?" He asked, eyes lighting up as they met hers.

"I guess?" She said, squinting at him, "Is this your version of a last supper?"

"Very funny, Bunny," He chuckled, grinning and leaning forward to brush his nose against hers.

They got out of bed, he put on pajama pants, and they found their way down to the kitchen. Demetrius got to work preparing coffee from a machine on the counter. Hopefully, it would be enough to soothe her aching head.

Bunny watched him with mild interest. He grabbed two mugs and the two stood in an admittedly comfortable silence for a couple of minutes before both cups were ready and he began preparing them.

Previously, she watched halfheartedly, but something caught her attention; he was measuring everything he was using. Demetrius didn't strike her as the bodybuilding type, so she couldn't help but wonder.

"Why are you so… *exact*?" Bunny asked, wrinkling her nose.

"What do you mean?" He responded, looking up at her absentmindedly.

"The coffees. You just measured everything that went into them. Why don't you live a little and add another splash of milk?"

"Bunny, are you seriously telling somebody else to live a little right now?"

"Can you just answer the question?" She said, exasperated.

"I think it's important to be exact, even in your everyday life. It makes me feel safe, Bunny, just like I make you feel safe." His tone said the conversation was over, and Bunny took the hint, even as she let loose a 'hmph' at the last part.

She wondered if he was any good in the kitchen, curious as to whether or not Demetrius had life skills. To pass the time while she waited to find out, Bunny busied herself by flipping through a cookbook on the island she was perched in front of.

When he placed the coffee in front of her, their hands brushed and Demetrius paused for a moment. Bunny felt her heart flutter. He gently held her chin between his pointer finger and thumb, turning her toward him.

They kissed deeply, slowly, blissfully. Bunny could feel her body readying itself for round two by the time he let her come up for air. She gasped for a breath and then stared at him, a flush flaring across her face.

"That's my girl," He murmured into her mouth as he pulled her back for another heavy session. Her arms encircled his neck, while his hands held her waist. This wasn't what she was expecting for the morning. Bunny figured she would have been sent home by now.

"I'm not your girl," She whispered back, and he laughed.

Demetrius made his way back to the counter and began taking out the necessary bowls and pans to prep whatever he was making. Bunny squeezed her thighs together in a huff and flipped a little more aggressively through the cookbook. She was desperate to not admit how badly she wanted him again. All she could think about was the feeling of his tongue doing unspeakable things to unmentionable places.

Starting, she looked up as Demetrius cleared his throat to get her attention. "How do you like your omelets?"

"Plain. Cheese, if you have it," She responded, elbow resting on the island, cheek in hand. Bunny was restless, horny, hungry, and had a headache. It was a terrible combination. Demetrius turned back to what he was doing and began prepping ingredients.

She cocked her head and watched, having never seen an omelet prepared the way he was doing it.

"What's the electric mixer for?" She inquired.

"Peaking whites."

Alright, he doesn't like to be bothered while cooking. Fair enough, she thought before turning back to the cookbook. There were a few banger recipes she wanted to remember to take photos of when she had her phone.

After he had finished cooking and slid the omelets onto their plates, Demetrius walked over to her with a fork in hand. He cupped his hand under her chin and lifted it, offering the utensil to her lips. Bunny locked onto his gaze and blushed deeply; there was something strangely sensual about what he was doing, an intimacy created between them.

As she took the bite into her mouth, she immediately realized that the man had life skills, perhaps better than her own. He could cook. Bunny swallowed and then said, "It was good, thanks," while looking anywhere but at him.

"Eyes on me, baby girl," He whispered.

She obeyed. She wet her lips. She prayed for strength.

"Come sit at the table," Was all he said as he turned and walked away.

Bunny followed him, padding behind Demetrius like a puppy.

Chapter 9

It had been three days since she had seen him. Bunny had dodged every encounter, declined every call, and made herself scarce. Especially today. She had a date tonight, and she didn't want to think about her latest mistake.

It didn't matter how much she couldn't stop thinking about his tongue, or his fingers, or his manhood. She shoved the thoughts deep inside just like she wanted to shove… *No, stop it. Absolutely not, Bunny,* she thought to herself helplessly.

Mark was actually a genuinely nice guy, probably one of the nicest she had ever met. Unfortunately, he was also unbearably dull. The man seemed to do very little outside of academia and the occasional non-fiction book. Hobbies and passions excited Bunny. She didn't want to discount somebody purely for not having them… but she wasn't above it, either.

Still, she wanted to give him a chance. If it led anywhere, it would piss Demetrius off. Besides, she had already given one lost puppy a chance. She might as well see if the other was any better.

Bunny was wearing a pair of jean shorts that were a little too short and a crop top that was a little too see-through. Recently, she'd gone out and bought a few pieces for her wardrobe that were more casual. It was about time, and she had extra spending money due to giving a few lessons at the barn. She wore natural makeup, and chose simple white sandals to top off the look. Normally, she'd bring a jacket, but the weather was supposed to be unusually warm.

The hallway was clear of giggling girls gossiping about God knew what. For this, Bunny was grateful. She was always pulled into these circles and found herself hopelessly lost. This wasn't because she thought less of them for their topics; Bunny recognized gossip and small talk as both necessary. They were cornerstones of human interaction. This was something she had learned during her sociology classes. Disavowing these critical parts of social bonding was rooted deep in misogyny.

The issue was with Bunny herself.

Her anxiety had not gotten better. She often felt that she was going to crawl out of her skin over the past few days. Bunny could barely concentrate on anything that anybody was saying. It wasn't just a genetic flaw, either. This time, it was situational.

There were too many things spinning wildly out of her control. She needed to let Katarina know she wasn't interested in the horse… or her son, but she'd likely leave that part out. She was also giving more lessons and providing hard labor at the barn to pay off the expense of Brianna helping her find a horse. Her college courses were getting harder, and she was falling behind in almost every aspect of her life. Bunny realized that she was near the cafe and pushed the flurry of thoughts behind the partition in her mind, hiding them away until later when she could be alone.

When she rounded the corner of the building, Mark was there with a small bouquet. They were beautiful, but she wasn't a fan of gifts that came with responsibilities. Floral arrangements always ended up in the trash because she'd never been able to keep anything green alive, and not for lack of trying.

He smiled and she returned it. They walked into the cafe, his hand on her lower back as he guided her to the line.

And then she felt eyes.

Bunny turned, scanning the area behind her. She smelled him before she saw him. Demetrius was standing not twenty feet away, smiling sweetly. It was a cloying sweetness, however, and it made her shudder.

Blue-green met black and they sat locked onto each other. Her heart began racing. Was he fucking following her now? It couldn't be a coincidence he was at this specific coffee shop. His house was on the other side of the town, and there were plenty of other options between there and the store they were in.

Not wanting to encourage him, she whipped back around. Mark finally seemed to take notice that her attention had been pulled away.

"Is everything okay?" He asked earnestly, smiling warmly at her. She smiled back and confirmed that everything was, in fact, okay. But she still stole glances over her shoulder now and then. She wasn't able to catch sight of him again, but Bunny could swear that he was still somewhere close by.

They placed their orders and stood off to the side. Bunny was too nervous to eat now. She loved the crepes here, but her stomach was turning at the thought of Demetrius doing something drastic. She didn't think he was the type, but women had been wrong about men far too often before.

For the rest of the date, she played it cool, but Mark played it hot. She had to keep his wandering hands in constant check as the warmth between her thighs signaled her arousal for a different man altogether.

They spoke awkwardly, Bunny always initiating and getting very little in response. It was frustrating and she wanted things to be over. So, she told Mark she had to be at the barn early the next morning for work.

He walked her home, the bouquet clutched in her hands and his jacket over her shoulders. He had offered it since she hadn't brought hers and the evening had turned cool despite the weather report. She still hadn't seen a trace of Demetrius since she met his eyes in the cafe.

When they got to her dorm a few minutes later, she spotted him. He was following them, now leaning against the wall at the mouth of an alley, staring her down. Bunny made purposeful eye contact, held his gaze, and then looked back at Mark, who was oblivious as per usual.

"Hey, do you want to come up?" She asked, positively vibrating at the prospect of rubbing it in Demetrius' face. He blinked, mouth slightly ajar, and then nodded his head. She smiled, took his hand, and led him in after touching her pass to the door scanner.

Mark's mouth was mostly limp, and Bunny didn't like the way he tasted when his weakly searching tongue slipped into her mouth.

She broke the kiss, pressing her lips to Mark's neck while her fingers curled in his hair. It wasn't unpleasant, and she'd see it through…
But it came nowhere near to what he had done to her. Not even close.

Bunny moaned unconvincingly, and he slipped inside of her finally. They had been wriggling around on the bed naked for God knew how long. He was moderately sized, enough so that she felt pleasurably full when his cock was in her to the hilt. Her hips tilted and she ground herself into him, gasping when a warmth began pooling in her stomach.

It wasn't an orgasm. No, it was just pleasure at its most mediocre. Mark was thrusting his hips awkwardly, gasping and panting in her ear in the most aggravating way possible. She decided to take over.

Twisting herself and pulling him with her, she whispered, "Let me get on top," as she made the motion. Mark agreed wholeheartedly and flipped them over the rest of the way. Bunny sat up straight and began rocking and circling her hips.

She closed her eyes and ran her fingertips across her clit, mouth opening slightly as she hit every point inside of herself where pleasure bloomed in full. And then, she closed her eyes. All she could envision was Demetrius; his smoldering, deep eyes staring out at her from the shadows, their predatory gleam tracking her, his tongue running up his finger…

Mark's voice faded to nothing, his pleas for her to slow down before he came early going unheard. She didn't care. She was about to come, and that was far more important to her than his stamina.

She panted heavily, moaning, before exploding around him, jerking as each shockwave of pleasure pounded through her body. Mark had also found his climax, gripping her hips tightly and tensing his entire body as he gasped and groaned.

When it was over, Bunny told him he should leave. Mark didn't argue. He got dressed, kissed her cheek, and told her he wanted to see her again. *Yeah, I don't doubt that…* Bunny thought to herself.

Briefly, she considered playing with herself. There was still a burning need between her legs that had her shifting uncomfortably. Unfortunately, she wasn't sure she'd be able to extinguish that flame. Bunny shuddered as she remembered the way Demetrius looked at her while they fucked.

That's what was missing. Demetrius had a genuine desire to please her, and make her come.

Mark cared only for his own needs.

She was failing to settle herself. Bunny pushed herself out of bed and stumbled over to her messenger bag. She pulled out the ibuprofen bottle, took two of the Ativan, and washed them down with water off the table the bag lay on.

It kicked in within an hour. Bunny finally fell asleep.

Chapter 10

So, here she was again. His mansion. Bunny shifted uncomfortably. This time, she was wearing a black turtleneck, tweed skirt, black tights, and loafers. Her hair was pulled into a no-nonsense ponytail. She looked like she was ready for an afternoon tea in Oxford, not a grimy college party.

Now more popular in the dorm because of her access to the Ivanov household, Bunny was accompanied by a troupe of five other women she barely knew. She didn't care. If a few giggling underclassmen made Demetrius' life harder, she would be all the more satisfied with herself. He should be aware that inviting one tends to attract others. Women didn't go to parties alone.

She hadn't seen him since the coffee

shop incident. Part of the reason she agreed to accompany her friends was because she wanted to gauge his reaction. She needed to know how the display had affected him. Bunny was playing a dangerous game.

He must not have been that angry because the group slipped through the front door without a hassle. They immediately split up and Bunny perched herself up by a window in the back with a drink.

She felt his eyes almost immediately.

When she refused to turn and look at him, smoke and cedar filled the air and she felt his mouth at her ear, "Come." The command was clear and she felt her breath catch in her throat from either arousal or offense. She was beginning to doubt she could tell the difference with him.

She followed Demetrius into the same hallway from the first party. Slipping inside one of the rooms, he grabbed her and pulled her in, shutting the door behind her.

At that moment, she could taste the bitter tang of fear coating her tongue and throat.

This large man was angry with her; she could practically feel it vibrating off of his body. And she was alone with him.

Bunny made a move for the door.

Demetrius blocked her way.

She shoved him.

He didn't move.

"Do you have any fucking idea how it felt? Watching you hang all over him?" He growled, teeth bared as his lips curled.

"I don't care, Demetrius. How you feel is how you feel," She hissed back, putting her face in his, "Besides, you don't have a reason to be angry. I'm not your fucking girl." At that, his nostrils flared and he stood up straight. Demetrius towered over her.

"I'm going to fucking ruin you, Bunny. I'm going to fuck you until you cry. I'm going to make you come until you're begging me to stop,"

Bunny felt her heart skip several beats while her pussy began beating a steady rhythm. She took a step back, unsure of where his anger would lead. Words were one thing, but the threat of physicality scared her far more. It felt like she was on a precipice of danger, edging slowly in the wrong direction.

His hand lifted and he grabbed the back of her neck with it, pulling her to him. Bunny bumped into his chest with a squeak and looked up, stunned. She was expecting an act of violence, not this soft embrace with his hand massaging the back of her neck.

"Bunny, I would never hurt you in anger, darling," He whispered, cradling her as she stilled in the comfort of his arms. She wasn't sure what to say to him. It was true that part of her feared his rage might turn physical, but half of her wanted that to be the case. Demetrius squeezed her tight and kissed her temple. Bunny whimpered and buried her head into his chest. "I'm sorry," she whispered, voice muffled. In response, Demetrius began stroking her hair, before speaking.

"Oh, you will be, Bunny. I have some things planned for you next time we play." His words crashed into her like an iceberg; there was far more to what he said hiding just beneath the surface. She didn't know what he had in store, but Bunny could feel herself growing wet between her legs at the thought of his wicked machinations.

"I shouldn't even be apologizing..."

She murmured, eyes closed, "I'm not your girl, Demetrius."

"Mmm… consider me convinced," He chuckled back, rocking her slowly back and forth. She hated how safe she felt, how protected. He cleared his throat gently before continuing.

"Remember that night we slept together? The morning after? That's the happiest I've ever been, Bunny. Standing in that kitchen making breakfast after fucking the living daylights out of you the night before. Waking up to you next to me was the closest thing to a religious experience I'll ever have."

Bunny was at a loss for words. She wanted to confirm that she felt the same, that maybe her heart beat in time with his whenever they were close, that maybe she wanted to curl into his arms and never leave that safe, warm place. But she didn't have the words. She never did.

"I don't understand. Why? Why me?" She was exasperated. The question had been weighing on her since he began his quest to conquer her.

"Because you're different, Bunny. There's some intangible quality about you that I can't put into words. You're smart, you're funny, and you're gorgeous. You're the entire package. And I think, on some level, you know that. I like the confidence, even if under the surface you struggle greatly with that trait." She shifted uncomfortably before changing the topic.

"You're not going to hurt Mark, are you?"

"No. But we should actually go take care of that." She didn't have a chance to question him. He was out the door and she was scrambling to keep up with him as he strode through the hall.

Demetrius burst back into the main room, and Bunny hoped that this bash wasn't about to turn into a bashing. While he didn't strike her as the violent type, there was something dangerous in the way Demetrius moved, something distinctly predatory.

He walked directly up to Mark, who was talking to what Bunny knew to be two of his friends and grabbed him by the shirt collar. Lifting him against the wall, Demetrius leaned into his face and said loudly, "Hey, Mark, I'm so glad I managed to catch you here." The other man was stunned, and his friends didn't seem to know what to do, either. They weren't about to put their hands on Demetrius Ivanov in his own home.

Or any other home, for that matter.

"You see that bitch right there? The redhead? She belongs to me, Mark. If I ever see you put your hands on my bitch again, I'll fucking kill you. Do you understand?"

Bunny's jaw dropped in disbelief. In that moment she would have dropped her panties, too, if it had been appropriate. There was something deeply attractive about watching two potential mates duke it out for their right to take you, even if she railed against the principle of it.

Once Demetrius had given his little speech, he let go of Mark's shirt and backed up a couple of steps. The entire party had essentially come to a standstill as everybody stood and waited for Demetrius to take a swing. The moment never came.

Instead, he told everybody to get the fuck out and that the party was over. There was groaning, pushback and a lot of disappointment. Bunny stayed behind. In some part of her mind, she wondered if the party had simply been a snare to snatch her, a trap laid so he could get his hands on her again.

Chapter 11

When the last of the people were gone, Demetrius led Bunny up to his room.

"So, do your parents just not care?" Bunny asked, thinking of the mess in the rooms below them.

"They're normally traveling. This is more my house at this point than theirs," He was fluffing up the pillows, and she was braiding her hair in front of the floor-length mirror, sitting cross-legged on the floor.

"That's why mom is trying to sell that horse. She's downsizing the herd because she just doesn't have time anymore."

"Did you ride as a kid?"

"I did, yeah. It was the best way to spend time with my mom growing up."

"Why did you stop?"

"I'm not sure. I think I just outgrew it."

Bunny finished braiding and turned her head to look at him. He was lying back on the bed now, book open and ready. She realized she must have been keeping him from it. As a reader, she had the decency to feel bad. As a brat, she had the need to bother him further.

"So, who cleans up after? We both know it's not you," She fingered the end of her braid, looking at him out of the corner of her accusatory eye.

"I clean up after myself, Bunny," His tone was softly scolding, "But Michael and the cleaners take care of things after a party."

"Who's Michael?"

"My best friend since childhood."

"Why haven't I met him?

"You have."

"No, I haven't."

"Do you remember that guy who busted in on us? The first night?"

"That's Michael?!"

"Yes, that was Michael."

Bunny wrinkled her nose as she remembered the interaction. She disliked the man immediately on instinct, and that was a hard thing to forget. He'd also been rude to her. She told Demetrius as much.

"How funny, Bunny, because Michael had something very similar to say about you."

"Who do you like more? Me or Michael?"

"Are you fucking serious?"

Bunny crawled over to the bed, grinning. Demetrius spun so his feet were on the floor and he was looking down at her.

"Tell me!" She whined as she put her folded arms in his lap and looked up at him through thick lashes.

"Bunny, this is so childish," Demetrius laughed, eyes crinkling. But then, his demeanor changed. She froze as the familiar gleam returned, much like when a cat spots a mouse. They sat, caught in each other. Finally, Demetrius spoke.

"I have to get you on your knees for me more often," The words fell from his mouth, barely a whisper. Bunny had to lean forward to hear him. When she registered what he was saying there was an immediate physical response, something primal answering the call of his passion.

Immediately, she was dripping with desire.

But she wouldn't be dissuaded. Bunny grinned, crawling into his lap so her knees were on either side of his hips. She wrapped her arms around his neck, putting her nose close to his, and then said, "So, who do you like better? Me or Michael?"

Demetrius snapped out of the spell he was under, eyes switching from glazed to alert. He groaned, leaned forward, kissed her, and then buried his face into her neck. Bunny giggled, grinding herself against him.

"You have to answer the question!"

"I'm not dignifying that with a response," Demetrius sighed, rolling his eyes and fighting the smile that threatened to betray his levity. His breathing was growing steadily heavier as she ground her core into his lap. Bunny could feel his manhood harden under her movements.

"How about you don't get anything from me until you answer?" She said in the most sultry tone she could muster, becoming more purposeful in the way she rocked her hips. Bunny pushed her chest up so it was crowding his face. Demetrius stiffened, his breathing now fully strained.

"I'm warning you, Bunny…" His voice was low and dark; an edge existed that hadn't been there before.

But it didn't dissuade her. It thrilled her.

"About what, Demetrius? What are you going to do about it?"

"If you keep it up, you can find out."

"Maybe I want to."

"I don't think you do."

Their eyes locked after the exchange and Demetrius leaned forward slightly, his face directly in hers. Within a few heartbeats, chaos broke out. Bunny was off his lap and running across the room. Demetrius was hot on her trail. He grabbed her and tossed them both to the floor, landing on his back with her on top of him. She squealed and yelped and began struggling against him.

With a grunt, he rolled over so she was crushed under his weight on her stomach. Bunny gasped and bucked her hips up, the only part of her she could freely move. Demetrius moaned in her ear.

"Get off of me," She screamed, bucking her hips again, this time with a little more effort.

"Do you want to use your safeword, Bunny?" He growled into her ear.

"Fuck you," She spat back.

"Well, alright!" He said, and she imagined he would clap his hands together if he could.

She felt herself sitting up as he gathered her into a bear hug. Her legs were folded under her, and the skirt had bunched up, leaving her bare. The tightness of his arms brought juxtaposing emotions to the surface; she was safe, but she was scared. Bunny panted, shivering and silent outside of her desperate breathing.

"I think you've been horribly behaved lately, my little Bunny," His arms tightened, "And I absolutely won't let you think it's acceptable." Bunny moaned softly as his molten tone washed over her. It was like a hot wave of water, soaking her panties as it crashed. This was bliss.

And then his hand came around her throat.

Bunny blacked out.

Chapter 12

When she returned to her senses, the world felt soft and sinister. She couldn't quite put her finger on what had happened. The past few minutes were a blur of color and fear. She was panting heavily. And shaking, she realized. And crying.

Fat, hot tears trailed down her face, eyes wide and unseeing even as her surroundings came back into focus. She remembered in that moment: he had grabbed her neck. Bunny whimpered and her sobs picked up speed when she recollected how it had felt. Her hand rose to lightly touch her windpipe.

That simple gesture, while done in good faith, had transported her back in time, yanking memories out of the darkest pockets of her mind.

She hated people touching her throat. She had never told him.

Demetrius… She thought faintly, realizing she couldn't feel him as her brain and body began to come back to each other. Bunny looked down and immediately gasped in horror. Her hands were smeared with trace amounts of blood. She was certain it wasn't hers. Lifting from her hands and knees into a kneeling position, her eyes were transfixed to her hands. Shaking, Bunny's head rotated until she could just see him out of the corner of her eye.

"Bunny, baby, are you back?" His voice was even and quiet, hands outstretched slightly, face unreadable to her.

"What did I do?" She sobbed, looking back at her hands.

"I think you had a really bad panic attack," He responded, coming a little bit closer to her. She noticed scratches up and down his forearms. Some of them still bled a little.

"I'm sorry, Oh, God, I'm so sorry," She started, shaking her head back and forth and covering her mouth with the back of her hand. The swirl of color and sound was settling and she could remember vaguely how his skin had torn under her nails while panic ripped her apart.

"Sweetheart, it's okay, I promise," He said, transfixed on her face, "Come here."

Instead of fighting him, she crawled over jerkily. She felt mechanical, like something inorganic. Demetrius gathered her in his arms, holding her tight to his chest. She hugged one of his biceps. He kissed the crown of her head.

"What happened, honey Bunny?" He whispered, rocking her slightly, sitting cross-legged so he could pull her into his lap.

"I have PTSD," She choked out, shame burning like fire through her chest and cheeks. She didn't tell people. She didn't want them to know. When people knew, it changed how they viewed you. Bunny was so tired of being turned into an "other" by the reality of her past.

"Why didn't you tell me what your triggers are?" He asked, voice high.

"Because it's none of your business."

"My blood on your hands would beg to differ," He scoffed.

"Okay, fine. I don't know. I just don't do that."

"Bunny, if you want to play with me, you have to be completely upfront with me. Do you understand?"

She shot up, almost smacking the back of her head into his face as she did so. Demetrius swung himself out of the way and met her gaze, aggravation clear in his.

"I'm sorry, but *who* wants to play with *who*? You've been hunting me like it's a sport for goddamn months!" Her arms were crossed. Demetrius sighed. He eyed her for a second before reaching out and taking her hands in his.

"Listen, Bunny, why don't we do some exposure? It might help. That was a pretty over-the-top reaction."

"What do you mean?" She said, shifting away from him slightly.

"I mean that we can work slowly toward me being able to touch your neck, even if nobody else can. You've been okay with me touching the back of it, so I think it's just an issue with the front."

She gulped, looking away again. He squeezed her hands and waited patiently while she weighed the options.

"How?" Her voice was soft and cracking.

"We just start around the area and slowly work our way toward it until you get anxious. We focus on getting closer and closer, as slowly as you need us to."

Bunny sniffled and nodded her head, still staring off into the distance.

"Let's get into a bath first," He said, eyeing her hands and his arms.

Chapter 13

They spent an hour in the tub, toying with different angles he could touch her from, and how much panic that positioning would inspire. Demetrius was gentle, slow, and checking in with her almost too much. Sometimes she wished he would just grab her by the throat and they could duke it out until she got over it. Demetrius had laughed when she'd relayed this and said that flooding her wasn't the answer.

Afterward, they stood next to his bed. She wore another one of his large shirts. Bunny watched him passively, unsure where the events of the evening had left them.

"How do you know me so well?" She asked, cocking her head to the side.

She took the two steps necessary to walk into his

outstretched arms as soon as he extended them.

"Oh, I've been watching you longer than you know, Bunny," He said, tightening the embrace, one hand around her waist, the other around the back of her neck. He breathed her in softly before continuing.

"Do you remember when you were a freshman? The party where you poured your drink on that dude and charged him like a wild animal?"

"Oh, God, not that," She groaned into his shoulder.

"Oh, he had it coming for sure. But that's not what made me look. You came into that party dressed like you were trying to get into a boardroom, not hang out with a bunch of college kids. I'll never forget it. You stuck out like a sore thumb. But you're gorgeous, so, like, it didn't even matter. Everybody was all over you. I didn't date freshmen, so I stayed clear, but I couldn't keep my eyes off of you. I had to know more." Bunny felt a sense of unease as he spoke, as though something ancient inside of her was screaming to run far away from this man. Against her better judgment, she ignored it and decided to be snarky.

"So, is this where you admit you've been painstakingly stalking me over the years to get me into this exact position with you?"

Demetrius laughed into her hair, his hot breath steaming her wet scalp.

"No, Bunny, not exactly. I stayed away from you because I don't date younger usually. But I couldn't get you out of my head. I would watch you from time to time, yes. I even started going with my mother to shows just to catch a glimpse of you in the ring."

"Okay, so how didn't I ever notice?"

"You never notice anything except what you want to. It's one of your many shining qualities. You have a wonderful talent for not seeing anything you don't want to."

She pushed back a little, stepping away from him, "And what the hell does that mean?"

"Bunny, please don't do this."

"Do what, Demetrius?"

"As soon as you feel even a little emotionally vulnerable, you turn it into an argument. Or you just get vicious."

"Maybe if you weren't so soft, you could take the blows," Bunny hissed in response.

"This is it. This is your problem."

"What? Tell me, Demetrius. Tell me my problem. I'd be absolutely fascinated to hear your theory."

"You're just so goddamn mean all the time!"

"What, so you're mad at me for being mean? What are you? Five?" She sniffed, crossing her arms.

"That's the issue, Bunny, that's the entire fucking issue," Demetrius choked out, "You're mean. You're mean to your friends, you're mean to people who haven't done anything to you, you're mean to me, and, most of all, you're mean to yourself."

Bunny blanched. He was hitting too close to home, and her heart ached with the fear of his verbal artillery. Her lower lip quivered. They stared at each other for a few moments before a tear rolled down her cheek and he rushed forward to hold her in a crushing hug.

"Why are you so afraid of being loved, Bunny?" Demetrius murmured into her forehead before shifting to kiss her temple, "You're always waiting for the other foot to drop. But it's not going to, baby, I promise."

And there she was, sobbing hysterically

into his shoulder once again while he held her close and crooned sweet, loving things into her ear. He was right and it hurt. There was a deep, horrible ache that fought and clawed to be seen, and she took every opportunity to squash it. The beast refused to be barred up in her chest forever.

This was the culmination of years, a release of tension that had built every time she had to cry alone. This man was promising her the only thing she had ever really wanted: home in another person. Even though she had no reason to think it, Bunny believed wholeheartedly that Demetrius somehow knew what she was releasing. She shook with the strength of her cries, clutching onto him like he was the only thing left in her world.

Because he was.

"Hush, baby," He whispered, holding her so tightly she felt like she was molded into him. Demetrius rocked her and loved her through every dip and peak as she was wracked with violent sobs.

Bunny's breathing leveled out, and she lay cradled in his arms like a small child. She looked up at him through tired, drooping eyes. Demetrius smiled back reassuringly, dropping his head to brush his nose against hers.

"Before you sleep, we need to do something we should have done already."

"Hmm?" She responded quizzically.

"We're going to fill out a couple of sheets. It'll let me know what your limits are and what you're comfortable with."

Bunny was alert now, her tear-stained face turned up to look at him. He leaned down to kiss her forehead before turning and walking to his desk. He pulled open a drawer and drew two pieces of paper from it before turning and walking back to her.

Taking her hand in his, Demetrius led her to the bed, motioning for her to sit next to him. She complied, still looking at him with a puzzled expression. When he handed her one of the papers, she looked down at it. It had three cells across and several down the page. Two at the top were labeled: hard limit, soft limit, on limits. The left-most boxes spanning down the page had what seemed to be different kinks and sexual acts. Bunny looked over at him, an eyebrow arched.

"This is for me so that I know where your limits are and what you want to engage with. It's just as critical as the safeword we established."

"Alright…" She responded, looking back down and reading some of the words. Some caught her eye: degradation, group sex, and anal play. A bright blush spread across her pale face, making her cheeks burn.

Demetrius barked in laughter, placing a hand on her thigh. She tried to quell the rising agitation as she went back to reading.

"If you're okay with doing it, Bunny, you have to be okay with talking about it. That's how this works. It's how it has to work."

Bunny shot him a venomous glare, huffing as she took a pen he offered to her, plucked from his bedside table. The weight of it in her hand felt like so much more than just metal and ink; it was the determiner of their deranged sex life.

Without a word, she began flying down the page, quickly ticking boxes with a certainty she didn't realize she had. To her surprise, almost everything was on limits for her. Just thinking about some of it made her stomach flutter with the stirrings of desire.

He watched her approvingly, smiling gently whenever she'd glance his way.

Once she was done, she handed the paper back to him, and he handed her the second one.

It was much the same, with different kinks and acts listed. Bunny made quick work of that one, as well.

"You know, you should probably be putting more thought into this, honey Bunny."

"Shut up and read. I know what I want."

Demetrius snorted, lips twisting into an amused smile that made the corners of his eyes crinkle. She felt her face redden again and looked away. He was beautiful when he smiled like that and, in her experience thus far, she had been the only one to make it happen. A long, low whistle cut the silence and she jumped, head whipping over to him. He was staring at her from half-lidded eyes, breathing deep and heavy. The flutter between her legs slowly morphed into a more insistent pounding.

"What is it?" She asked softly, meeting his gaze.

"You're just the most beautiful thing I've ever seen, and I can't wait to do all of this"—He gestured with the paper—"to you."

Bunny sucked in a sharp breath, and then whispered, "Fire hydrant." Immediately, his gaze softened. Demetrius turned, placing the papers on the bedside table once more, and then leaned forward so that their noses were touching.

"Good girl using your safeword," He whispered, bringing a hand up to her cheek, cupping it softly before he pulled her in for a gentle kiss.

Even though lighting shot through her core at his words, Bunny's mind didn't lend the right mood to engage with him sexually. She just wanted to curl up and go to sleep.

"Alright, my love. I think we should turn in for the night."

She agreed, he turned off the light, and they climbed into bed. Bunny sighed contentedly as she fell asleep, snuggled into his chest.

Chapter 14

Bunny had woken up early, this time not surprised to find herself in Demetrius' bed. She had then gone to her dorm to get ready, gone to the barn, worked for eight hours, and then made her way back to Demetrius' house. Today was free of classes for her. She wasn't even sure why she was doing this to herself. The constant driving and activity were exhausting.

Parked in his driveway, she crossed her hands over her steering wheel, before leaning her forehead against them. Her breathing was even and steady as she considered the situation she had gotten herself into.

This wouldn't work. It couldn't work. She hadn't met his parents, but Bunny knew they would never approve. She came from far lesser means, and her family was unsavory, to say the least. No, they would likely want what every wealthy family desires: a perfect match for their most prized possession, their only son.

There was also the issue of who Demetrius was as a person. She didn't know him very well. This had all started for him years ago, apparently. For Bunny, it had only been a couple of weeks at best, and a couple of days if she was being realistic. She gritted her teeth as she fought to stop spiraling.

Her entire body ached. She wanted a long, hot bath and a massage… Both of which she might be able to get from the smooth-talking idiot inside. She realized this with a smile and decided to get it over with. He had texted her that he had a surprise tonight.

Once inside, she walked up the stairs to get to his room. Bunny ran a bath almost immediately, stripping out of her barn clothing. She had brought an overnight bag filled with the necessities this time. It was clear she wouldn't be leaving before sunrise at this point. Bunny put a leg over the tub to test the water. It was perfect, so she slid into it slowly, letting the steaming heat comfort her aching body. She lay weightless, breathing evenly, focusing on maintaining a clear mind.

And then it was there: smoke and cedar.

She opened her eyes just barely and saw a shadowy figure sitting on the edge of the tub. It would have scared her if she hadn't known by scent that it was Demetrius. Bunny smiled slightly and then sat up in the tub. Demetrius reached out to cup her cheek.

"Hello, honey Bunny," He whispered, leaning forward to capture her mouth in his. She returned the gesture, moaning slowly as he incorporated his tongue into the dance. Heat pooled between her legs and she reached a hand out to stroke his cock. Demetrius stopped her. She pulled away to question him, and he hushed her, placing her hand back in the water.

"You'll see, darling. I have a surprise planned."

She wasn't sure what he meant by that, but Bunny was certain she was going to love it. Or hate it so much that she loved it, at least.

When she came down the stairs in her

bralette and shorts, she stopped with a start. There was another man there, somebody she wasn't sure she had met before. Bunny smiled weakly at him, looking over at Demetrius. He shrugged and smirked.

"My friend Jeremy wanted to come over, baby. Come hang out with us? Just for a little bit?"

She continued down the steps to where Demetrius outstretched his arms and embraced her. The three headed down to the basement. Bunny had expressed previously that she thought the nickname for the room was stupid. "The Chill Room" seemed ridiculously juvenile.

She had learned then that it came from his childhood. Michael had called it by that name because his own home was far less chill. Whenever he needed a place to stay, he'd live with Demetrius and they'd spend their time in the basement, playing video games. They came from families of similar means, but, from what she'd heard, Michael had a much rougher childhood. The sob story did little to endear him to her, but it did soften her attitude a touch.

As they descended the stairs, Bunny walked between them; behind Jeremy, in front of Demetrius. The room came into view and she was surprised to see it was already set up for guests. There were even a slew of drugs spread out on the coffee table.

Jeremy must be somebody important to him, she thought to herself. She looked over at Demetrius, but he was busy pouring wine into a decanter. "It needs to breathe, Jeremy," He was saying, "Like most things."

Jeremy smiled, reaching past Demetrius for the entire bottle. "Come now, Demetrius," He responded, "You know that's all bullshit. We'll pass the bottle around. Besides, I know how much you like to share."

The way he said the last part made Bunny feel wary, especially when he turned to look directly at her. She swallowed heavily but didn't hesitate when Demetrius led her back to the couch. They sat at the innermost point, and she immediately went to the tray of goodies. She plucked a bean up and looked at him inquisitively.

"Molly and coke, probably."

That was all she needed to hear. Bunny snatched the credit card on the table and smashed the pill under it with her palm. From there, she cut a thick line and blew it. The drip was immediately what she could only describe as, 'nasty as hell.' Demetrius laughed, taking the tray away from her.

"I think that's quite enough, honey Bun'."

"I think that's quite enough of you trying to shorten my already short nickname," She said before snorting in a distinctly unladylike way.

"If you're done making cokehead noises over there, take this," Jeremy called out, leaning over and handing her the bottle of wine. She took a deep swig, but the taste was ruined by the post-nasal drip. She passed it to Demetrius.

As she suspected, the two men fell into easy conversation, ignoring her almost completely. The only reminder of his affection was a hand he had wrapped lightly around the curve of her waist. He was tugging her to him. She scooted in. Before she knew it, he had laid into the curve of the couch, pulling her with him. She laid on her back, letting her head fall back as she soaked in his embrace.

Chapter 15

Bunny could feel the molly working its magic. Demetrius was lying beneath her, and his pleasant warmth radiated into her back. Her head was up by his, and one of his hands was rubbing her stomach gently. Jeremy sat on the other lounge of the U-shaped sectional. He was laughing a little, talking with Demetrius while Bunny lay in abject bliss. She wasn't listening.

She also wasn't paying attention to where his wandering hand was traveling. Soon, he had cupped one of her breasts and used his thumb to rub her nipple through her bralette. Bunny began whimpering, tingling with the need to be touched by something, anything. Her body was begging for his hands.

"That's my girl, Bunny," Demetrius

whispered, his other hand moving to her hair, gathering it and holding his fist to the base of her neck. The pull on her scalp felt incredible.

He was gentle and slow, watching for signs of discomfort and allowing her time to decide if this was something she wanted or not. She had never been touched like this in front of another person before, but something inside of her yearned for more.

His restless hand began pushing downward and, before she could say anything, slipped under her shorts and dipped beneath her panty line. Bunny whimpered as he began to play with her clit. She was soaring, somewhere far above herself, and all she could feel was the warmth of him and the rough brush of his fingers against her most sensitive places.

Jeremy had gotten up and took a few steps, kneeling so that he was beside Bunny's legs. "May I?"

Demetrius shifted so his calves crossed over her shins, and pried her legs apart, holding them in place.

"What type of host would I be if I didn't let you sample the most divine offering I have?" Her blood ran cold, a furious shiver building at the base of her spine. He was offering her to his friend like a glass of wine. She felt the cool air between her legs as Jeremy unbuttoned her shorts and pulled them off of her.

He moved between her legs as Demetrius moved his own out of the way. The man locked his eyes on hers, kissed one of her thighs, and then slid off her panties by hooking a finger through the crotch and slowly dragging. Once they were on the ground, Jeremy ran his tongue up her slit. Bunny was frozen in place. Her pussy was thrumming, a powerful need tightening her core until her desire became painful. The room froze…

Until she let her head fall back and moaned. At this signal, Jeremy quickly began incorporating his fingers, working her exactly how Demetrius would. She briefly wondered if they had planned this. They must have. Bunny gasped for breath and let out a series of mewls while Demetrius slipped both hands into her bralette and began playing with her nipples. Her hands gripped the bottom of either side of his shirt. Her knees had lifted, pressing her pussy into Jeremy's face.

"Oh g-god," She whimpered into

Demetrius' neck, her head whipping from side to side as each shockwave of pleasure rippled through her. Then, she felt a hand between her ass and Demetrius' clothed cock. It began moving, and she realized that Jeremy was stroking Demetrius.

Bunny began panting, rocking her hips in time with Jeremy's spinning, thrusting fingers. His tongue was relentless, as were his lips.

"That's it, baby, just like that," Demetrius' mouth whispered next to hers, "You're perfect. You're doing so good for me," This was punctuated with a kiss on the corner of her mouth. Bunny whimpered and buried her face into his neck, hands flexing as rapture radiated through her entire body. Before she could stop herself, Bunny was spinning out of control, her body jerking as she cried out pitifully. The peak of her climax hit ruthlessly.

"You were doing so good, baby, what happened?" Demetrius chuckled into her ear, the hardness pressed against her ass, evidence of his arousal. She briefly wondered who it was caused by: her or Jeremy? It was likely both. The salacious thought made her giddy.

"You can leave now, Jeremy," Demetrius

said dismissively, hand gently wrapping around the side of Bunny's neck and face nestled in her hair.

"But I-"

"Get out."

Jeremy had started to argue, but the response from Demetrius was enough to make him think better of it. He quickly took his exit.

"And you…" He breathed out as she panted and whimpered in anticipation, "You, my darling, have earned yourself quite the punishment for embarrassing me in front of my friend." Bunny's throat tightened, her face burning with the memory of Demetrius holding her while she was grinding her pussy into the face of another man.

But, goddamn, if it wasn't hot.

She was sure she'd pay the price for coming without asking, and the thought of that made her even slicker. Bunny watched him stand up, and he extended his hand.

"Come with me."

Chapter 16

He had walked her up the stairs toward his room. She hated that she already knew the layout of his house well enough to know where in the maze he was headed, even as she felt turned around.

Once they arrived at their destination, Demetrius walked directly to his bed, leading her there. He directed her to lie on her stomach. Bunny complied without complaint, eagerly awaiting whatever he had decided to dole out.

When he returned with lube and a toy, she felt her heart skip a couple of beats. The events of the night had already worn her out, and this next part would surely be a test of her stamina.

She had the power of molly and coke to carry her through, however. And, with any luck, she could sleep through the comedown.

He placed everything on the bed next to her. Bunny knew that his smoldering eyes were watching. Demetrius kneeled behind her, coated two fingers in lube, and slipped them inside of her ass.

Bunny bucked with a gasp, her head shooting up. Demetrius grabbed the back of her neck and pinned her back down, his fingers scissoring and spinning and thrusting. Bunny lay frozen until she felt him jostling with his pants. She glanced over her shoulder to see he'd taken his cock out and was positioning it.

Demetrius started hushing her when he leaned forward. Bunny felt herself groan and give in, finding his rhythm and following it, massaging her rear entrance with the tip of his cock. Demetrius grabbed Bunny's hair and yanked her head back with his free hand.

"Do you want this cock, little Bunny?" He growled, teeth on her neck.

"No," She squeaked in response.

"Too bad."

And with that, he was sliding inside of her tightness, and Bunny was crying out in a heady mix of pain and pleasure as he sank to the hilt.

He didn't start thrusting right away, however. Instead, he grabbed the vibrator he had brought over and turned it on. Bunny whimpered beneath him as he slid his hand between her in the bed, bringing the toy to press against her clit.

The pressure of their crushing bodies drove the toy into her most sensitive point almost painfully.

She was yowling now, writhing beneath him and begging him- to what? To stop? To keep going? She wasn't sure, but she couldn't keep the pleas from coming. Demetrius slowly moved his hips, dragging himself in and out of her leisurely.

"Can- can I c-come?" She managed to stammer.

Demetrius murmured, "Of course, baby. I want to hear you scream for me."

And she did. Bunny's cries ripped through her throat and out of her mouth at a volume she wasn't sure she was capable of under different circumstances. The fire in her veins set her body ablaze, and Bunny was separating from herself. It quickly burned out of control and she felt herself pulsing painfully under the crush of the vibrator.

"Demetrius, it's too much," She shrieked, shoving both hands under herself to grab at his forearm. She was unsuccessful in dislodging him. Bunny bucked and squirmed, desperate to find relief.

"Oh, God, please stop," She cried out, "I don't want this, Demetrius!"

"Liar," He growled back. She fought until sweat slicked her hair back and her throat was raw from protest. He was right. She did want it, desperately so. If she didn't, she would call out her safeword and he'd stop immediately. There was something endlessly sensual about asking this man to stop and having him push her to the next plane of pleasure even in the face of her begging.

Bunny froze as her entire body tensed, desperate to turn in on herself, to get away from the merciless crush of the vibrator against her clit. Demetrius was still slowly pulling out and sinking into her ass. She was spinning blindly in a world of black spots and watercolored snapshots. Even in this state, she knew she could reach for her safeword.

But she didn't want to. Not yet.

The vibrator was removed, and he was leaning forward to whisper in her ear, "Bunny, baby, are you okay? Do you want to keep going?" She moaned, "I need it. Please."

"Do you remember your safe word?" Another tender whisper.

"Yes," Another whimpering moan, "Please, just fuck me. Fuck me so hard, Demetrius."

With no further urging needed, he shifted back so that he was kneeling behind her, grabbed her hips, and began slamming himself into her. Demetrius pulled her back to meet every thrust, and Bunny screamed into the pillows.

He just felt so *good*.

"Fuck, baby, I'm g-going-" He was whimpering. Demetrius was whimpering for her. Bunny felt herself in freefall once again while Demetrius came powerfully inside of her. They both jerked and rocked as a climax ripped through their bodies. When it was over, he laid on top of her, face in the middle of her back.

"Holy shit," He groaned.

"Yeah," She breathed.

The next morning, Bunny had questions.

"Why did you let another man do that to me?" She asked, propping herself up on her elbows to look at him over the fluffy duvet. Demetrius stared at her for a moment before he smiled and said, "Because I like the power trip. I let him get a taste, but who ended up fucking you to pieces last night? Who left with a rock-hard cock and no relief?"

Bunny felt a tiny shudder run through her body at the thought. Her mind kept reaching back toward the memory of looking down from Demetrius' arms while another man ran his tongue over her most sensitive places. It was strange. Bunny hadn't often thought about sex beyond what it felt like. Porn didn't interest her, and she only fucked with the lights off and under covers usually.

Seeing that man ravage her, seeing the real mechanics of it, had excited something in her. She snapped out of her thoughts and fired her next question at him.

"Okay. You didn't get off the first time we had sex? Why?"

"Because you needed me more than I needed to empty my balls."

He reached a hand forward and wrapped it around the back of her neck, yanking her forward so she landed across his body. Bunny huffed but shifted into a comfortable position. Demetrius continued, "Back to the first question. Think about it like this: it's like allowing the pack to take a bite before the alpha runs them off to eat his fill, y'know?"

"I'm not sure that's how wolf packs work," Bunny said flatly.

"And I'm positive it was an understandable analogy regardless."

She couldn't help herself. She smiled.

"That's my girl," He grinned and ran the back of his pointer finger down her face. They stayed like that for a little bit before getting out of bed and getting into the bathroom. Both of them were sticky and disgusting from the previous night's play.

Afterward, Bunny stood naked in front of the mirror. Demetrius walked up behind her and held her around the waist. He smiled at her in the reflection before saying, "Y'know, Bunny, I think someday I'll have to pass you around my associates like a party favor. Put a little collar on that pretty neck and let them get a taste of what I have."

Her eyes widened visibly and she pulled in a deep breath. Bunny had never considered anything along those lines before, but that didn't stop her from thinking it sounded hot as fuck. But on principle, it made her balk. It felt wrong to want something so dirty.

Demetrius raised his eyebrows. Then, his eyes closed to slits while his mouth curled into a vicious grin. "Oh, Bunny, I think you liked that, didn't you?"

He squeezed her hips and kissed her neck before continuing, "Do you want that? For me to pass you around, never quite letting you get off? Letting every person in the room edge you until you're begging for anybody to take you over the edge?" One of his hands slipped down so it was gripping her inner thigh, just next to the apex of her legs.

"How about I pass you around my group of friends instead?" She snapped, pushing his hands off of her hips and crossing her arms.

"Would that make you happy?" There was a genuine quality to his voice, "Because if it would, Bunny, I would do that for you."

She admitted begrudgingly that it wouldn't but she was still offended he'd even suggest something like that to her. Demetrius smiled knowingly and the conversation moved along to other topics.

Chapter 17

"So, you do want to sleep with a woman?" Demetrius asked, brow furrowed while trying to understand what she was saying.

"Yes! I mean, maybe? I don't know. I've fantasized about it, but it's always seemed so scary," Bunny leaned forward and revealed the information in a conspiratorial tone, as though they were in the midst of scheming a grand heist, not talking about sexual preferences.

The conversation had come up because she had finally gotten the nerve to question him about what Jeremy had been doing with his hand while he ate her out. Demetrius had quickly offered a simple explanation: he was beginning to jerk him off. She had blanched at this, dumbfounded by the idea that Demetrius would let another man touch his cock, let alone stroke him to completion.

He countered that sex felt good and, so long as it was consensual, he was open to different experiences. It sounded so responsible and mature when he said it that she almost forgot he was talking about another man making him come. Bunny giggled, shaking her head a little bit, as she considered the concept.

"Toxic masculinity is a serious topic, Bunny," he had said, crossing his arms.

And now, they were digging into her reservations about sleeping with another woman. She said she wasn't sure she'd like pussy. He told her that it wasn't a necessary component of sleeping with a woman– just ask most men.

She'd laughed sourly, thinking about her own past partners who all had their own excuses. Bunny still hadn't told Demetrius he was the first to use his tongue and mouth to pleasure her, even further convinced at this point that it would make him far too smug to bear.

Bunny had also brought up how it would be horribly difficult to find a woman she'd want to sleep with. She was notoriously picky about everything and that extended to her sexual partners unless she was feeling particularly self-destructive.

"I really want a redhead, y'know? Somebody with a slender build and nice tits, but not too big," She began listing out attributes like she was making a grocery list, and Demetrius snorted.

"So, you basically want to fuck yourself?" He said, eyebrows raised. Bunny had hit him with a pillow, but she hadn't disagreed.

They were both giggling by the end of it, holding each other in their arms. Bunny had never felt safe like this, both emotionally and physically. She had scarcely found them separately. Together? Previously, she would have said that was impossible.

Demetrius had been staring at her for a few moments when she finally looked up at him and said, "What?"

"Nothing. I just can't stop thinking about how beautiful you are when you can't decide if you're scared of me or not."

"I thought you didn't want me to be scared of you?" Her confusion was clear.

"No, I don't want you to be genuinely afraid of me, Bunny. But I do love seeing how much you look like a scared, little rabbit when I'm about to put you over my knee."

Her pussy began to flutter at the mention of it, breathing speeding up just a touch. He was right. Whenever she was about to be punished, dread filled her in a way that only highlighted the surge of pleasure.

"I think I like being afraid of you," She said, snuggling into his chest.

"I think what you like is experiencing fear in a controlled, safe environment."

"Calm down, Google MD."

"No, I mean it, Bunny. With the PTSD, it's hard to face fear as an emotion. When you're with me, you can let yourself be afraid while knowing you're safe. I think it's therapeutic for you."

She chewed on her lip as she considered what he said. It was a solid theory and one she couldn't disagree with. But she wasn't about to admit it. Sensing her apprehension, Demetrius leaned up, kissing the top of her head.

"Alright, let's go do some shots. I'm feeling a little flirty," He purred, nuzzling her neck.

"Oh, my God. Never say that again," Bunny replied, pushing his face away.

Chapter 18

They stood in the kitchen with a bottle of whiskey and a glass between them. At first, they each took a shot and stood there. Then, Bunny suggested a drinking game: Answer or Drink. She was sure there were probably a bunch like it, but she had come up with the idea her freshman year with a group of friends. You were asked a question and had to either answer it or take a shot. It got chaotic quickly and was always a good, messy time.

"Why do you have daddy issues?" She slurred a little, laughing as she said it, already three shots in.

"I do not have daddy issues," He laughed back, looking at her in disbelief.

"Yes, you do. Answer me or drink, bitch."

"Alright, fine. He just wasn't around a whole lot. I'm afraid of disappointing him. What other stereotypical bullshit do you want me to spew before you're happy?"

"That'll do, actually."

"Great. So, why do you have daddy issues?"

Bunny started at that, her face falling. She hadn't even considered the possibility that this could be turned back on her. Demetrius reached out and touched her hand.

"You don't have to answer that, Bunny. Or drink. I'd prefer it if you didn't, actually. I think we've both had enough."

She didn't make eye contact with him as he took the bottle she had picked up from her grasp, and went to put it back on the bar cart. Bunny was lost in thought, trying to stave off how uncomfortable she felt.

Demetrius walked back, grabbing her hand and leading her out through the kitchen and into the garden. From there, they walked toward the barn but stopped halfway and took a right. This led them to a little firepit she hadn't noticed before, right on the edge of the woods. She didn't question him at any point.

"Run."

Bunny felt her heart drop. She took a step back nervously, unsure of his intent. *He cannot be serious. What's he going to do? Chase me through the woods?* She thought to herself, something akin to flame filling her lower belly at the concept. He wanted to hunt her down like a goddamn animal…

And then, as her clit began to pulse furiously, Bunny realized she loved it.

Demetrius repeated the command with a deeper tone, taking a step toward her. She gulped, and then turned to take off. The fluffy moss and soft, muddy ground would prove powerful opponents to her movements. However, they would also help her avoid banging up her feet too badly.

Fear took over when she heard him crashing through the undergrowth behind her. Bunny began running blindly, branches whipping her while she worked her way toward… Well, somewhere. She had never been in these woods, let alone at night.

She soon lost him. She was sure it was by design; he would be close, biding his time. With this thought, she spotted some large boulders and decided to camp out using them as coverage. If he knew where she was, she could try and sprint away. If he was just a touch too far away, he'd likely walk right past her. It would then be a question of who was hunting who.

Her feet were covered in grime, but she hardly took notice. The squish of mud between her toes became background noise as she made her way through the trees carefully, hunched over and breathing as softly as she could through her mouth, trying desperately not to pant for breath. Bunny could feel sweat cooling on her skin even as she burned with the effort expended during her run. Adrenaline pumped heavily through her body tinged with trepidation. The combination was intoxicating. The heavy buzz of whiskey settled heavily in her veins, relaxing her even while her heart raced.

Something shifted behind her, and Bunny jerked with a yelp when she felt an arm around her midsection. "Boo," Demetrius said into her ear before biting at it gently. Bunny, on instinct, threw her head back. She felt a thud, heard him grunt in pain, and then took off. He had grazed her earlobe with his teeth when she threw her head forward and the skin stung.

Suddenly, it was no longer a game for her. The interaction had activated her fight or flight reflex and she was tearing through the woods, desperately trying to stay away from the danger chasing her down.

But she could hear him closing in behind.

Demetrius allowed for a good, long chase before he overtook her, tackling her to the ground. Bunny was breathing hard with effort, her muscles straining as she attempted to fight him off. Demetrius wrapped his hand around her neck before he growled, "Stop fighting."

His voice was deep and dark and angry. Bunny stilled immediately. It took her a few moments to settle into his hand, still getting used to trusting the sensation. Her pussy began to throb in time with her pounding heart and she felt a war stirring in her mind. She was terrified; the blood in her veins was glacial. However, she was also impossibly hot for him.

Demetrius turned her around.

The expression he wore had a wildness to it, some lupine quality she had noticed distantly before. Now it was at the forefront and Demetrius wore a wolfish grin. He wanted to devour her. Bunny felt the firm reassurance of his hand around her throat and leaned into it. It made her feel safe, even despite the outright threat it presented. But Demetrius always had a way of making her feel secure even in the most tense moments between them. This always started with her being unsure about her throat being touched and ended with a deep appreciation for it.

He pushed her to the dirt, holding her there while he took in her body with raking eyes.

"Holy shit."

His voice wavered, shaking with the force of his emotions. There was a reverence in his eyes now and Bunny blushed under the gaze he reserved for when he worshiped her. She felt distinctly undeserving of his attention and yet called to it all at the same time. Bunny squeezed her eyes closed and worked on controlling her heavy breathing.

"No, baby. Look at me," Demetrius purred, and her eyes snapped open on command, wide and staring into his. Blue-green met black and sparks flew; her pussy was positively sore with need.

"You're safe," He whispered, resting on his shins and knees over her while he brought his free hand up to smooth back her hair and cup her face, brushing his fingers across her cheek as he did.

She felt her lip quiver. Something inside of her was breaking as he held her gaze, his eyes full of passion and adoration. Bunny didn't think anybody had ever looked at her the way that Demetrius did. It was like he saw something inside of her that nobody had cared to see before.

He leaned down to capture her lips as a tear fell sideways down her cheek, running across her temple and landing in the shell of her ear. She kissed him back softly, following his lead lazily as they lay on the forest floor. It smelled like fresh soil and bright greenery.

"Let's go home," He whispered, tickling her ear. Bunny giggled.

"That's not my home, Demetrius," She scoffed.

"No, but *I am*," He responded. Before Bunny could respond, he had pressed his mouth to hers again.

Chapter 19

The next morning, she woke up to the sound of arguing. Bunny shot out of bed, immediately pulling on clothing as quietly as she could. She wasn't sure what was going on downstairs, and she wasn't about to make her presence known.

It sounded a lot like his parents were home.

Once dressed, Bunny crept over to the door and pressed her ear to it. She could make out the muffled shouting of what sounded like an older man in what she assumed was Russian. Upon hearing "nyet", the only Russian word she knew, Bunny was sure of it.

There was a pounding on what she assumed to be the stairs. She flew across the room and slid into the walk-in closet just before the door opened. Peeking around the corner, she realized it was just Demetrius.

He sat on the bed, elbows on his knees and face in his hands. He seemed absolutely defeated by whatever conversation he had just engaged in. She heard him let loose a low groan.

Bunny wasn't sure what to do; she had never seen Demetrius in such a state. She wasn't sure he could be moved to brokenness. *Maybe that's how he feels about me...* The thought was fleeting yet she felt something "click" in her brain.

If that was the case, maybe he'd want the same approach she did.

Bunny climbed onto the bed and laid on her side behind him. Using insistent arms, she pulled him down toward her until she was cradling his head against her chest. Demetrius had closed his eyes softly and was breathing slowly.

"I'm filled with doubt, Bunny," His murmur startled her, "But the one thing I don't doubt is my ability to love you the way you need to be loved."

She sucked in sharply, holding her breath

as she digested what Demetrius had said. It was true. He could. If that was his saving grace, Bunny could consider herself a hero in his eyes. For a few moments, he was silent, but then he began speaking to her in a soft, even tone.

"The reason I live here is because they need somebody to watch the house. They're never home, so it's actually great most of the time. But my father and I don't generally see eye to eye. He wasn't upset that I brought you here, or that you've been essentially living here," He eyed her and she bit back the reply she had lined up. Demetrius shifted, then picked up where he left off.

"He was upset because I hadn't mentioned you to them. He thinks I'm hiding things. I keep telling him that I'm an adult and I don't need to report back with every event," He laughed.

"What's funny about it?" She scoffed, actively repulsed by the notion of her parents keeping tabs on her. She couldn't imagine what that was like, especially with the activities Demetrius was actually up to in his parent's home.

"It's actually kind of endearing. They just miss me, you know? I'll have my own place soon.

They're going to retire to France and this house will be rented out within the next couple of months.

"That's… a lot. France. Wow," She responded, tensing beneath him.

"I'm not moving to France with them, Bunny," He said, pinching the bridge of her nose. He had turned to face her. She pulled back and gasped softly. Demetrius laughed again.

"But they're going to miss me a lot more when they're in another country permanently, y'know? He's just worried about losing touch. We'll be summering in France next summer, by the way."

"Who the fuck is 'we'?"

"You and me."

"Absolutely not."

"Bunny, France is beautiful."

"I'm not debating that."

"Then come with me."

"I meant I'm not debating whether I'm coming or not, but especially not based on the beauty of the place," She eyed him and then continued in an exasperated tone, "Demetrius, I can't afford that! I'm horse shopping, and also going to Europe is a very expensive thing to do."

He let out a hearty laugh and squeezed her tight. Once he had his laughter under control, he nuzzled her neck and whispered, "Bunny, you wouldn't be paying for anything. You're mine, so I'm taking you with me. Think of yourself as luggage."

She gasped and then let out a shriek of disapproval, shoving him. Even so, she couldn't stop the bubble of laughter that rose from her. She was flushed once again.

"I am not luggage, Demetrius," She said, smacking his arm, "And even if I was, not even you could afford that price tag."

"Let me buy you a Birkin and we'll talk about price tags."

"Demetrius, I'm serious. I'm not doing this with you."

"We'll talk about it later," With this, he sat up and hushed her. He was listening intently. In a couple of seconds, he yelled something in rough gibberish, which is what Bunny had decided Russian sounded like. She had jumped, startled by his sudden outburst.

Demetrius pulled her to him and kissed her neck.

"Easy, angel," His breath brushed her

neck gently as he spoke just millimeters from her skin, "My mother was trying to listen at the door so I yelled at her." He winced before continuing, "I really need to move out, my God."

He got out of bed and walked over to his dresser, taking care of small grooming tasks; spritzing cologne, fixing his hair, performing small rituals that seemed to finish the steadying that Bunny had started. Something caught her eye she hadn't noticed before and she stood, walking over to him.

"Ooh, what's this?" Her sing-song voice was overshadowed by the rattle of a bottle. It was opaque, white. Demetrius turned around with a raised eyebrow before his face sank upon seeing the bottle in her hand. He immediately went to snatch it from her.

"Don't grab things from me!" She laughed, dancing out of the way. But then she saw the look in his eyes, and that stopped her dead in her tracks. Demetrius snatched the bottle from her and stormed back over to his desk, where he put it down firmly.

Bunny started toward him, but he pushed past her to go sit on the opposite side of the bed.

His back was to her, and she knew his

head was in his hands again without looking to see. She wasn't sure what had happened. Bunny wasn't trying to upset him. It was just a pill bottle, like every other one they handled while passing out party favors when his friends were over.

"Demetrius, I didn't know…" She started, moving her way toward him like he was-
A frightened animal, She realized, sucking in a breath. Was this it, then? Was this how he felt when she had her little meltdowns and forced him to pick up her pieces? Bunny swallowed down her guilt before moving to his side. She knelt beside the bed and put her head on his knee.

"Leave it alone, Bunny," He muttered, "I'm not upset. I'm just exhausted. The last couple of weeks have been… a lot."

"Can we at least talk about it? Because I don't understand why you're so upset. And I want to, Demetrius. I promise I do."

For once, Bunny sounded sincere. Her heart ached for this side of him.

"I was diagnosed with Obsessive Compulsive Disorder at 15, but I had early-onset symptoms that came in around 10. The medication you picked up was Abilify. It's not strictly for OCD, but it's used for severe depression, which I also have when I'm unmedicated. For some reason, a lot of people with OCD say it helps. I'm one of those people."

She said nothing, allowing the silence to coax out more information. This was more about him in a few sentences than she had learned over the past few months. Bunny hated herself for how hungry she was to hear about how he hurt. It was as though some sick part of her was convinced their broken pieces could fit together at all the jagged seams.

"The intrusive thoughts became… too much. It was a lot, Bunny. I ended up in an inpatient facility for intensive treatment. I put in the work and had an excellent care team. Now I'm in therapy once a month and take medication. Fully recovered. That's really all there is to it."

"I think there's more," Bunny said softly, pushing on his knee so she could stand up in one movement. She crawled onto the bed and sat behind him, pressing her body into his.

She was coming to realize why he knew so much about how to deal with her issues. At first, she had wondered, but now it made sense. Bunny had no idea he had struggled in any way, let alone such an intangible one that she knew little to nothing about.

"Yeah, maybe there's more," He said, taking his face out of his hands, "But I don't want to talk about it right now. Not with that going on." He tilted his head toward the door.

"Well, what do we do now?" She asked, squeezing her arms around his waist.

"We are going to go downstairs and have breakfast with them."

"No."

"What?"

"Oh my God, you can't just spring this on me!" She said, panicking at the concept, "Demetrius, I only have that slutty, little outfit I was going to wear today for you. They can't see me in that!"

"You're fine, Bunny." He laughed, reaching forward to cup her face, "They'll just think you're one of the vapid models I bring around sometimes."

Her face darkened immediately, eyes sharp and trained on his. Demetrius swallowed nervously.

"When is sometimes?" Bunny's tone was sharp. Demetrius suddenly realized why she was upset.

"Oh, wow. You're jealous," He said, puzzled by the idea.

"I'm absolutely not," She sniffed, glancing away from him, "I just want to make sure you aren't going to give me any diseases since you've apparently been banging random bitches."

"Whatever, Bunny. Get ready. Now," His last word was growled out when she opened her mouth to argue. Instead, she walked off with a huff to the bathroom with her overnight bag. It was fine, she could handle breakfast with his parents.

Chapter 20

Breakfast was already mostly set by the time they made their way downstairs. Bunny had a pair of tiny jean shorts on but had borrowed one of his pull-over sweaters so she didn't look quite so exposed. She had managed to style it so that it looked presentable. It was thankfully cool enough to justify the heavier top.

Bunny took a seat next to Demetrius at the urging of his parents. She tried not to make it obvious but she was absolutely observing both of them. They fascinated her.

Katarina was a woman with a thick build who Bunny could only describe as "overtly fabulous." It wasn't necessarily a flashing of her wealth. Instead, she simply wore loud, bright colors. Bunny had the feeling she made a statement whenever she entered a room without so much as uttering a word.

His father was a tall, large man who looked like he had never laughed a day in his life. His face was set into a grave expression, outside of minuscule shows of emotion when Katarina addressed him.

They turned and started fussing over Bunny.

"Oh, so beautiful! Your hair!" The thick accent made it clear that Katarina had not grown up as a native speaker. Bunny thought the way she spoke was absolutely lovely.

"Make beautiful babies," His father agreed solemnly. Bunny choked on her water. Demetrius groaned. Katarina slapped her husband's arm.

"Go, go! Go make yourself useful," She crowed, shooing him away. Once Demetrius' father had headed back into the kitchen, Katarina looked at Bunny.

"I am so sorry. He is not so good with words, you know?" Her voice was pleading but lighthearted, as though she were trying to keep her cool in the face of near disaster.

"Oh, no, it's okay," She said, trying her

best to keep a straight face. Demetrius was the one flushed this time. She was no stranger to embarrassing parents, and this didn't bother her in the least. She got comments wherever she went on her hair, and people had often brought up her having red-haired babies.

Like many others, it was a rudeness you learned to live with.

His father returned carrying a tray of sausages and they all sat down. Bunny was delighted with the fare. Demetrius picked up her plate and began serving her, hovering over each option. She quickly realized what to do as his father did the same thing for Katarina, and she responded with "Yes" or "No."

It was the strangest thing she had ever experienced. Katarina must have noticed her confusion because she explained happily, "You must keep good woman happy, Bunny. Treat her like queen, so she can make you king. Boris made sure he knows that."

Bunny smiled weakly, eyeing what fork Demetrius had picked up and doing the same. There were multiple options. Why were there multiple options? They all did the same thing.

The rest of the breakfast passed with

pleasant conversation. Bunny was too nervous to eat too much, but she did manage half of what was on her plate. Katarina had invited her to come for a family trail ride. Bunny didn't have the heart to refuse.

So, she agreed.

The trail ride had been lovely. Bunny had ridden the little Sporthorse she had come to see the previous week. Demetrius looked mouthwatering in his riding gear.

His parents were pleasant, but loud and opinionated. She often found herself fighting a smile because they were being unintentionally hilarious. Demetrius would catch her gaze and she realized he was in the same boat. She felt a connection to him in those moments that were so much more intimate than sharing her body.

Afterward, they hung out in the barn, drinking and engaging in pleasant conversation. Bunny briefly realized that she was rubbing shoulders with her fuck buddy's parents and felt weird about it. Demetrius would not agree with her label, but she still wasn't ready to be his girl. There was something inside of her that still balked at the concept. She knew to accept him would be to accept ownership.

They kept asking if she was excited to join them in France. Bunny would stammer through answering, while side-eyeing the idiot who had told his parents a little more than he had admitted, apparently. To her disappointment, they were leaving the next day. She realized at that moment that she needed to go stay at her dorm that night. There was no way she'd let Demetrius continue believing she basically lived with him.

A little while later, they sat outside in the waning sunlight, a fire lit in the center of the seating area. They were in his father's garden. She was surprised when he had first said it. That felt like an eternity ago somehow. Boris was apparently gifted with a green thumb. When younger, he had spent years cultivating and nurturing the plants around them.

Bunny listened with rapt attention, loving every bit of information he offered on everything around them. He was like a talking encyclopedia, if somebody set the voice to "angry Russian father" instead of the nice British woman.

After a couple more hours, she felt herself starting to get sleepy. His mother commented fondly, crooning at Demetrius to bring Bunny to bed.

"The girl is tired, Demetrius, tsch," She said, waving an arm, "Go, go. Take her upstairs. Run her a bath."

He laughed in response and agreed. Bunny no longer wondered where he got his methodology for treating her from. She let him lead her back into the kitchen, and then all the way to his room. Before they left, his father barked something in Russian and Demetrius snapped back over his shoulder.

"I have to go, Demetrius," She whined, pressing her hands against his chest. He had been trying to convince her to stay for over an hour. It was a light tug-of-war between them; Demetrius was a dog with a rope toy.

"But you could just head to the barn from here, and it's closer!" He whined back in the same tone, grinning while pulling her closer.

"Demetrius…" She trailed off, staring up at him. Her feet felt like they were buried deep in wet cement and she was finding it hard to unstick herself from his grip. Admittedly, she wasn't trying very hard.

"I know how to fix this," He said gravely, leaning down and picking her up under her thighs. She yelped and jumped into his arms. Demetrius carried her over to the bed as she wiggled and protested loudly. He leaned down to drop her on her back, kissing her neck.

"Hush. Parents."

She shut her mouth instead of yelling at him, remembering that they weren't alone. The positive was that the proximity of his parents dampened the fire billowing in her belly. That was the hardest part about leaving. He made her horny, point blank.

The *bastard*.

Suddenly, he was smiling wickedly. She frowned, and then her eyes grew wide.

"Absolutely not-" She started, but she didn't get far. He had his hand between her legs and another clapped over her mouth.

"Better be quiet, baby," He whispered in her ear, "We wouldn't want you to sound like a whore, would we?"

Her eyes widened to saucers as she

slammed her legs together. It didn't deter him. Demetrius laughed and shoved a knee between her legs, prying them apart. In an instant, everything was forgotten. He was playing with her clit and she was laying there breathing heavily into his hand.

There was something insanely hot about him keeping her quiet while he fucked her with his fingers, using every trick possible to make her spin out of control while commanding her to be silent. Bunny was soon sweating and shivering, close to an orgasm but trying her hardest not to give in.

She couldn't ask him permission, for one thing. For another, she didn't think he deserved the reward.

Demetrius stopped. He withdrew his hand, kissed her cheek, and then flopped over on his back. Bunny blinked, sat up shakily, and looked at him with wide eyes. He didn't seem to take notice.

"What the fuck?!" She hissed quietly, face flushed and eyes bright with need.

"Well, I figured you'd want to get going, y'know?" He said pleasantly, smiling at her.

"Demetrius, I'll fucking kill you. I swear

on it."

"While my parents are here? For shame."

"Demetrius…" She ground his name out, eyes narrowed. She was now kneeling about a foot away from him. He simply leaned over to the other side to grab a book from the bedside table and opened it up.

Bunny pounced on him.

Chapter 21

The next morning, she was up bright and early. He had successfully gotten her to sleep in his bed and Bunny was grumbling about it the entire time she was getting ready to head to the barn.

He was right, though. It was technically closer than her dorm was. She drove further out, away from town, down curling roads that stretched into farmland. Within fifteen minutes, she arrived. Brianna was nowhere to be seen in the barn. She usually assumed Bunny had things covered and had since she had first started working at the barn. However, she wasn't sure if she had lost that privilege since she had been so unreliable lately.

She sighed and got to work.

There were five horses currently getting medication for ulcers, and two of them were on preventative treatment, as well. The timing had to be just right so that each animal was taken care of properly. You couldn't feed them for a certain period after each treatment. Bunny normally had five or six timers going at once to keep track.

After the medication was prepared and given, she began dropping feed for each horse using buckets that had been prepped the previous day. Each feed bucket swung out on a hinge, a feature she loved because it meant not having to go into the stall. Instead, she could whip down the aisle. It took around an hour to get everybody fed and out into the pastures. In that time, Brianna showed up, walking up to Bunny with a coffee in each hand. She smiled at Brianna, taking it from her.

"So, you want to explain what's been going on?" Brianna asked directly, giving her a look that suggested it wasn't a question at all.

"You want to ride about it?" Bunny responded, using a phrase they had coined when she was a teenager in the swings of puberty. There had been many long trail rides taken because Bunny just needed a breather and somebody to chat with.

"Absolutely."

Bunny rode Olive, a beautiful liver chestnut mare. To her right, Brianna had chosen her personal horse for the outing. He was a Friesian, one of the most recognizable breeds. Diego was jet black with thick feathering on his legs, mane, and tail both full and floating on the wind.

There was a reason Friesians were used so often in movies; they looked like something out of a fairytale.

"So, who's the boy?" Brianna asked, hands on the buckle of her reins as she sat back in the saddle and let Diego plod along. They were on a slow, leisurely walk, neither in the mood to push things along.

"That obvious?" Bunny winced, smiling weakly.

"Oh, sweetheart, you could not be clearer with all the bullshit you've been pulling. Is he staying at your place?"

"No, other way around, actually."

"Bunny!"

"Brianna!"

They laughed at each other, hands covering their mouths, mirrored behavior adapted after knowing each other for far too long.

"Alright, fine. He's just some dude who's been trying to chase me down for months. He's basically insane and I think I might be an idiot for being involved in… whatever we are," She said, pausing at the last part.

"And why do we not have a label yet?"

"Because of me."

"Mmm."

She winced a little again, the tone all too knowing. Brianna had firsthand experience with Bunny's inability to commit.

"What type of insane are we talking about?" Brianna said after a few moments, letting the silence grow between them comfortably before asking.

Bunny blushed, biting her bottom lip.

"Well, he's, uh… adventurous," She said slowly, trying to figure out how to tell Brianna about what she'd been up to without revealing the reality of the situation.

"What, like, in bed?"

"Yeah, something like that."

"That's not a bad thing. You're young! You should be experimenting."

Bunny smiled, dropping her feet from the stirrups and letting them hang long, rolling her ankles. If only Brianna knew the truth of what Demetrius has been doing to her.

She'd probably drop dead.

They rode on in silence, the stunning countryside stretching out as far as the eye could see. Softly swaying trees lined the path to either side, and Bunny was thankful for the breeze. It carried the scent of the coming autumn, her favorite season. There was something about the finality of the leaves turning and grass dying that appealed to Bunny.

Her puff vest was maroon, with her initials in gold thread on the right breast. The back of the vest had the stable's logo emblazoned. It was perfect for the weather, keeping her warm without making her sweat.

The boots she wore were relatively new. The stiffness of the leather made her ankles ache, and Bunny thought for a moment about how good Demetrius was at taking care of sore muscles.

She shifted uncomfortably in the saddle. "Look, Bunny," Brianna began, "I don't know what's going on with you and Mr. Mysterious, but I do know that you're glowing. You shouldn't be tied down all the time, y'know? You're a kid, for God's sake. So, get out there and have fun while you can. You deserve it after everything. Besides, who knows? He might be the one."

After finishing, she grinned, eyeing Bunny, who she knew full well didn't believe in the "one true love" nonsense.

"Don't give me that bullshit, Bri'," She groaned, letting her head fall back.

"I'm serious, though, Bunny. I want you to find your happiness. You haven't been this happy in a long time."

Chapter 22

Bunny's car had finally given up on her. She had known it needed maintenance of some sort, but she wasn't sure what, and she wasn't sure how to get it checked without running the risk of losing her horse ownership aspirations.

So, she decided to do some research herself… and promptly came up empty. Bunny was useless when it came to anything mechanical. Ignoring the odd noises had become a way of life as she accepted her fate. There was a difference, however, between strange sounds and a flat-out refusal to start. This was a terrible time for mechanical issues. She had to return home to get a critical document and had been dreading the drive, dreading the arrival, dreading the entire event.

The trees had all mostly shed their leaves, save for those that would stubbornly hold on all winter long. Bunny missed the bright foliage that autumn brought, especially when she drove along back roads that were only speckled with what once flourished.

She sighed, hanging her head, sitting in dejection. The hood was popped and her arms were crossed as she stared down at a bunch of junk she couldn't tell apart.

"Well, hello, little lady," A familiar voice said behind her, "Mind if I take a look?" Bunny started for a second but quickly realized who it was. She turned and offered a weak smile to Demetrius. He reached out and she jumped into his arms happily. Snuggled into his chest, she decided that maybe not being able to go home wouldn't be the worst thing. She would have more time to spend with him.

He was wearing a pair of khakis that she knew his ass would look great in just by the shape of them. His dark green half-zip sweater was soft under her bare hands. Underneath, he wore a white collared shirt. A brown belt topped it off. The thought of that belt sliding out of the loops flitted through her mind.

"Bunny, what are you doing, baby?" He asked, looking over her shoulder at the blue Subaru. She mumbled that she didn't know, and he laughed.

"Aren't you supposed to be going home?"

"Aren't you supposed to be magically fixing the car problem?"

"Are you asking me to buy you a new car?"

"Absolutely not, Demetrius."

"Do you need a ride?"

"Absolutely not, Demetrius."

They argued about it for a stretch, with him pushing hard on the idea of driving her. His angle was that they could get a hotel room and make a little vacation out of it. Her angle was that she didn't want her parents to have anything to do with her life.

"C'mon, Bunny," He whispered into her ear finally, kissing her temple after, "Let me in, baby."

At the mention of breakfast in bed after bondage all night, Bunny finally broke down and relented. She knew it was better to give in when he was being like this. She was never going to win.

He shut the hood while she grabbed her bags from the backseat of her car. Demetrius took them from her and they walked the short distance to where he had parked his new car. She opened the door, admiring the way everything moved so smoothly. It was a far cry from what she was used to. Curious, she had snuck onto the manufacturer's website and punched in for the best model there was. She couldn't imagine him getting anything less.

The price made her feel like she was going to have a panic attack.

She was only paying half that for the horse she was looking to buy, and even that felt like she was in a dream whenever the mention of the number came up. She never thought she'd be in a position to purchase an upper-level horse, let alone an import. She knew she'd never be in a position to buy that car.

Bunny slid into the seat and took out her phone. It was the one area where she splurged, buying it outright but spending a thousand or more for the newest model. Working under the table at the barn for extra cash and tutoring had earned her enough to justify the purchase.

It connected to the audio and she smiled

smugly to herself as Demetrius slid into the driver's seat. Glancing over and noticing her phone synced up, he groaned, knowing he was in for a ride full of haunting indie music he wasn't entirely in love with.

"Do we need to stop at your place?" She asked, crossing her legs and leaning over the console so she could touch his shoulder. Demetrius smiled indulgently at her, leaning down to kiss her chastely.

"No, I have an overnight bag in the trunk. Why would we stop?"

"Oh, I was just wondering," She sighed, fluttering her eyelashes.

"You absolute animal," He sighed through a smile as he smoothly drove the car out of the parking spot.

"We could pick up some stuff so we can play at the hotel…" The sentence drifted off and she ran a finger up and down his forearm. He took that hand off the wheel and buried it between her legs.

"Or we could go to a sex shop while we're on our little holiday. Think about it, Bunny. We can buy the weirdest shit they have, drop a solid grand, and they'll never guess we're doing anything but playing an expensive prank."

"That is the dumbest idea I've ever heard, Demetrius. They're going to know."

"How would they know?"

"Nobody is spending a thousand dollars on a prank, Demetrius!"

He laughed and placated her. For the rest of the drive, her haunting indie music played and he hummed along despite himself.

Chapter 23

They pulled up to his luxury apartment complex thirty minutes later. It was further out, and the commute was a strain on her. Demetrius stayed in her dorm as much as she came to his apartment.

It was incredible to Bunny, the support he received from his parents. She was floored when she found out that they paid for everything while he was pursuing an education. His parents wanted him to go to college and take over the family businesses. She hadn't really been listening beyond that point, however. Bunny was stuck on the part where he didn't have to lift a finger to survive.

She tried not to let it get to her. He didn't choose what he was born into any more than she had. Surprisingly, it wasn't the wealth that she lusted after. No, Bunny craved something more emotional than that. She was jealous of how supportive and wonderful Boris and Katarina were.

She waited for him to come around and open her door. There were certain things he expected of her, both as his girlfriend and as his submissive. She fingered the necklace she now wore daily.

Originally, Bunny had refused to accept the gift. But he insisted because it was how he was collaring her. After some convincing and a little roughhousing, she finally gave in to him. It was a beautiful, simple heart locket on a thick chain.

From Tiffany's.

It had been $12,000.

Bunny had taken two Ativan after finding out the price of the jewelry she wore around her neck daily. She would never get used to that. At this point, she couldn't imagine her life without him.

And it wasn't about the money.

No, Bunny wasn't an idiot. She knew women needed to have their own source of income at all times. A nest egg was a necessity in case things went sideways. She would get her degrees and secure her own funding, and Demetrius would never own her financially. He still insisted on treating her, often giving her very little room to refuse. It was a point of endless bickering.

They walked into the door, which opened by the courtesy of a doorman. It was another thing she'd never get used to. Demetrius passed him a few dollars as he passed, thanking him. Bunny hardly spoke to other people when with him now. She'd smile politely and allow him to take the lead.

It had done wonders for keeping her calm in public. Bunny would get overwhelmed sometimes, especially when she was symptomatic. He'd put his hand on the small of her back and guide her, taking care of conversation and excusing them as necessary.

They took the elevator to the penthouse.

Demetrius and Bunny had picked out a range of fun things to use… and some not-so-fun things, in her opinion. He was being mean to her, and likely because she had been so outright in her refusal to allow him to accompany her home. Hopefully, a taste of what was her childhood would deter him from ever wanting to set foot in that little town again.

When they turned onto the highway, Bunny shifted in her seat, suddenly feeling the weight of the decision she had made. Let me in, his words echoed in her mind. Was this really letting him in? Into where? It was a part of her past now, and she refused to see it in her future.

So, where did Demetrius fit back home?

No, not home, she thought to herself. Home was sitting next to her, happily driving into a hell he was in no way ready for. She wasn't sure he could ever be ready for it. Could anybody?

The journey was long. They stopped a few times for snacks but didn't want to take the time to sit down and eat. That was fine because Bunny loved feeding him while he drove. It always ended in her melting into giggles and him shouting.

It didn't scare her anymore. Demetrius could not scare her. She was certain this man would protect her under any circumstance, and she no longer saw him as a patient predator. No, she saw him as the protector he always was.

Chapter 24

Bunny swallowed hard as they pulled into the trailer park her parents now lived in. She had nothing against trailers, and she also knew that there were differences between the parks, just like anywhere else.

This was not a good park. She suddenly wished they weren't driving a gorgeous new car. Taking a shaky breath, she relayed the directions to him from her phone. She had texted her mother to ask for their new address. She had also texted her to let her know that Demetrius would be coming with her. She hadn't responded.

It wasn't a sure bet she had even gotten the text. *Jesus, I hope she did,* Bunny prayed internally. She was a staunch atheist. However, this seemed like an appropriate moment to beg for an act of God.

When they pulled up, she groaned. The grass hadn't been touched all season, leaving the scant front yard in disarray. Paint was peeling and one of the windows was smashed in. Or out. She wasn't sure.

"Why don't you stay out here?" She suggested, unbuckling and steeling herself for the showdown that was sure to occur as soon as she knocked on the door.

"No, I don't think I will," He said slowly, eyeing his surroundings. She groaned once more, this time internally, exasperated with his need to protect her. She didn't need protecting, especially not on a trip she had been going to make alone previously.

"Come on, Bunny," He said, slapping the steering wheel. He then turned and opened the door, stepping out, and Bunny scrambled to join him.

"Really, Demetrius, I just think you should-" She was cut off by a booming voice.

"Who the fuck are you?"

They both turned and a redheaded man was standing on the porch in a bathrobe, tighty whities, and sporting a shotgun.

"Holy shit!" Demetrius said, putting his hands up.

"Dad, what the fuck are you doing?" Bunny shrieked, throwing her hands out.

"Bunny, why didn't you tell us you'd be coming? It's getting late. Scared the shit out of me."

Her father was slurring his words, and she was sure he was drunk.

"Put the fucking gun away! Where's mom?" She said through a strained voice, looking away from her dad and putting her hands on her hips.

Demetrius was gaping like a fish as he looked between the two of them.

When he noticed her looking at him, he snapped out of the initial fear of seeing a mostly naked drunk man with a gun.

"Mr. Townsend, I'm-"

"I don't give a rat's ass who you are."

"Okay..." Demetrius sighed, clapping his hands together, "This is off to a really strong start, I think."

"Shut up," Bunny hissed at him quietly.

"Well, stop standing there. Come on in!" His voice wasn't necessarily inviting, but both Bunny and Demetrius started walking towards the rickety porch. As always, Demetrius held the door for her since her father was taking up the back.

"Oh, got yourself a fancy boy, huh?" Mr. Townsend's voice was a sneer, his mood shifting suddenly. He was turbulent at best when drinking. Bunny was used to it. Demetrius was unlikely to put up with it.

They were standing in a kitchen, shabby and filled to the brim with papers, mail, trash, and other items that had no place in the room. She was just relieved there wasn't a crack pipe laying out. Then again, the night had just begun. Her father put the gun away while Demetrius and Bunny stood, the former taking in his surroundings with a sense of awe.

"Mom?" She called out, poking her head around a hallway.

"What!" A shriek, obviously unhappy.

"I'm here for my paperwork!" She screamed back.

"You'll have to come back later. I don't have it."

"What the fuck do you mean you don't have it?"

"Don't talk to your fucking mother like that," Her dad barked, making Demetrius wince. He was standing in the corner, looking relatively small for once.

"Okay, I'm sorry, I'm sorry," Bunny placated the man, soothing him with an even tone. But afterward, she was calling down the hallway again.

"Mom, which room is it in? I'll just find it!"

"Fine, Barbara, whatever! Do what you want! In the little office. Have your father show you. And don't look through my shit like a nosy little bitch!"

Bunny rolled her eyes and turned to her father, who grunted and turned, showing her to the room as suggested by her mother. It was an absolute wreck. Boxes and papers were scattered everywhere. Bunny heaved a sigh and shut the door. She then sank to the floor and breathed heavily into her hands. Demetrius kneeled next to her and pulled her into his arms.

"It's okay, baby, we'll find it," He whispered, holding her close. Smoke and cedar wrapped around her like a hug, intensifying his embrace.

"I should have known she wouldn't have it for me," She whimpered, "I just wanted to believe her so badly. We're never finding it in this mess, Demetrius. We should just leave."

"Can you order it? What are you here for?"

"My birth certificate," She sniffled a little, eyes burning as tears threatened to come.

"Oh, honey Bunny, we can get another one of those by ordering it. You don't have to do any of this."

"Wait, really?"

"Yeah, it's not difficult, but it is a pain in the ass. Why the hell didn't you get it sooner?"

"My mother wanted to hold onto my birth certificate. I didn't want to fight her on it. She took it wherever it needed to go."

"Well, we'll get you a copy and fix things, baby," He said, kissing her on the top of the head.

He stood up, held out his hands, and she took them. Rising with his strength, Bunny took another look around the room, and then they left it. As soon as they got into the living room, her father started in.

"Who the fuck are you, anyway?" He

asked Demetrius.

"I'm her boyfriend. She hasn't told you about me?"

"The little bitch hardly bothers to phone home. The fuck do you think?"

She could tell that Demetrius was fighting to hold back his temper and losing the battle quickly. Bunny linked her arm through his so she could give him a gentle but insistent squeeze.

"Okay, I think we're going to leave now," She said evenly, leading Demetrius toward the door.

"Oh, so you just show up, don't even bother looking for whatever the fuck you think you need, and decide to leave? Not even going to try to have a fucking conversation? You've always been so ungrateful. We should have left you with those state people."

She sucked in a breath and felt Demetrius tense. She hadn't shared that bit of information with him. In fact, she had shared very little about her parents except that they weren't close and she had her reasons.

"Fuck you, you little bitch," He slurred, pointing at her, "Get the fuck out of my face." Bunny distantly realized she was nowhere near his face before all hell broke loose.

Her father lunged forward, raising his hand to strike her. She felt air whip by her as Demetrius finally lost his cool and shoved her father back with a force she hadn't seen him from before. Mr. Townsend stumbled back and hit the wall.

"Fuck you," The redheaded man roared before charging.

Demetrius swung and caught him clean across the face.

Bunny screamed.

Mr. Townsend was against the wall again, holding his face as blood gushed between his fingers. Even as she grabbed him to stop, Demetrius stormed forward and put his face close to the bleeding man's. His voice cracked like a whip.

"If you ever try to touch her again, I will kill you. I'm promising you that."

He then turned, wrapping an arm around Bunny, and led them out of the little trailer. She felt like her legs were made of lead. Her body was on autopilot, leading her through the motions as her emotions struggled to keep up with the pace. There was shouting and crashing behind them, and she knew her father would be losing his shit.

Her mother…

She pushed the thought out of her head. Where was the woman when he was coming after Bunny? She couldn't worry about somebody who should have protected her and didn't. She had learned at least that much in therapy. Demetrius opened the door, buckled her in, and dug through her purse for her ibuprofen bottle.

"He's not going to call the police, is he?" Demetrius questioned softly as he poured a pill into his palm and took a drink from the center console. He leaned forward, pushing the pill into her mouth, and then holding the straw up for her. She accepted the treatment mechanically, his voice drowning out in the softness her brain conjured cushioning the scene around her. Bunny was no longer within herself. She was floating somewhere far away, above the earth, separate from it all. She was beyond panic. This was something entirely numb and disconnected.

"No," She finally responded, her voice sounding far away, "He's probably got a warrant out."

It hardly registered when the car began

to back out and then finally made it back to the main road. Once the medication settled into her system, barely the whisper of an effect, she realized that things had gone significantly worse than she could have predicted.

"Pull over," She groaned.

"What?"

"Demetrius, I'm going to be sick, pull over."

He immediately complied, parking far into the shoulder of the road. She got out, sucking in deep breaths and trying to stave off the panic. He had seen all of that. The filth, the anger, the disregard for anything. She wasn't sure how she felt about him seeing that side of her life, but it felt like something tender inside of her had been exposed, and she was squirming in discomfort. She bent over at the knees and heard his door open distantly.

He stood a few feet away from her. Once the silence had stretched significantly, Demetrius spoke softly, "Bunny, please, don't feel embarrassed about-"

She cut him off sharply, voice rising, ringing with hysteria, "I'm not FUCKING EMBARASSED." Bunny covered her face with her hands, pressing the palms into her eyes. She gasped a couple of times in a desperate attempt to bring in more air.

"I'm not embarrassed and I wish people would stop assuming that," She choked out, "I'm fucking ANGRY. I'm angry they did this to me. I'm just so fucking angry," It trailed off into a sob and she felt her face burn. The shame threatened to spill over, her eyes filling with tears.

Demetrius wasn't taken aback by the outburst so much as the vehemence in her voice. She was prone to displays of temper but it was never backed by tears, or the intense sadness he could all but feel radiating off of her. He eased forward, a hand out. In this moment that hung between them like a sheet of glass, Bunny felt more fragile than she ever had. It was as though one wrong move could shatter her entirely.

She shied away from him, keeping a hand cupped over her mouth while the other waved him off. Out of respect, he obeyed the gesture and stood his ground. Bunny spun back toward Demetrius, sweeping past him toward the car. She got back in and curled up on the seat. She hated it, she decided. She hated that he had seen that side of her life.

Chapter 25

They drove without so much as a whisper from the car radio to distract them. Bunny had curled in on herself, sitting hunched with her elbow resting on the window, head cradled. Demetrius could hear the occasional sniffle from her.

Suddenly, a noise sounded through the silence like a clap of thunder. It was a genuine sob. Bunny had been trying to hold back, but the sharp pieces spearing her insides would not be ignored. These were not the type of tears that could be held back.

When Demetrius looked over, he saw that the thunder was backed by lightning— tears streaming freely down her scrunched-up face, hand now wrapped around her mouth again. She sucked in air through her fingers, vision wavering with shaking drops hanging onto her eyelashes, and those yet to well over onto her cheeks. So, she didn't notice at first when the car had pulled to the side of the road again.

And then, without ceremony, Demetrius was pulling her into an embrace. She gasped and pushed but he wouldn't be dissuaded this time. Bunny was too exhausted to fight, skin crawling with the lingering anxiety. She needed the pressure of his arms. So, she collapsed into Demetrius and buried her face in his chest. His scent surrounded her. It was a welcome distraction from her racing mind. Reaching for a solution, Bunny's brain started listing her senses and any currently stimulating factors for each.

Scent? Smoke and cedar. Touch? Strong arms. Sound? His voice. He's saying something. Sight? Nothing. Taste? Salt from the tears. She began to filter back into reality, grounding through the sheer force of her will until the haze receded far enough to listen instead of just hear.

"You're right, Bunny, they shouldn't have done that to you," Demetrius' voice was even and gentle, "They should have protected you. They should have loved you enough to take care of you. You should be angry. I would be pissed." The validation only made her sob harder. She felt his hand slip around the back of her neck, squeezing and releasing, thumb rubbing into the muscle on the side.

As her sobs subsided, Bunny stayed where she was. Demetrius made no move to push her away. Instead, they sat together in a thick silence. She heard him sigh before his lips barely brushed the shell of her ear as he leaned his head down, "Bunny, you're not stronger and you're not better for what happened. You're made of glass and it's starting to crack. But I promise I will always pick up those pieces, no matter how they slice me. I'm ready to bleed for you."

She took a sharp breath. She had never felt so seen than in that moment, so naked in front of him even while she still wore the heavy garments necessary to combat the chill in the air.

———————————————

When they finally showed up at the hotel, it was close to nine o'clock at night. Bunny felt like collapsing and never getting up again. Demetrius drove up to the front, coming around to help her out of the car.

"Mr. and Mrs. Ivanov?" A voice to her right. She assumed it was somebody affiliated with the hotel.

"Townsend," She said suddenly.

"I'm sorry?" The new voice questioned.

"Sorry, my poor Bunny isn't feeling well tonight," Demetrius flashed a stunning smile and wrapped his arm around her waist. Bunny gave him a look but said nothing else. The two men chatted as a driver took the car away, their bags unloaded onto a cart.

"I assume the kitchens are closed?" Demetrius asked briskly.

"Yes, but certain accommodations could be made, of course," The man responded.

They continued to chatter as they walked through the doors. Bunny hardly noticed any of it, glued to Demetrius and holding on for dear life. She was terrified she'd fall to the floor if he let go. Even so, the grandness of the place was not missed. Bunny knew he had expensive taste, but this was the nicest hotel she had ever seen. Part of her felt uncomfortable, her roots planting her far from these luscious fields he felt so at home in. She was just with the man who did belong to this world.

The next few minutes passed in a blur. Soon, Demetrius was holding her close in a luxury suite on the top floor. It had beautiful floor-to-ceiling windows that looked over a lake and forest. Light sparkled off the surface of the water, the dark waves twinkling as they crashed.

"Oh, my Bunny…" Demetrius had come up behind her and put his hands on her hips. She froze. He froze.

"Bunny, what's wrong?" A whisper in her ear.

"   Nothing," She whispered, eyes and mind still glazed with the effects of her medication. Suddenly, she was turned around, staring him in those intense eyes as he held her to his chest.

"Tell me. Now."

She could have moaned just at the tone of his voice. It had that velvety quality that made her legs quiver as wetness gathered between them. Bunny licked her lips before answering, shifting her eyes away from his.

"I just… don't want to talk about it, okay? I just want to pretend it didn't happen."

"But it did happen, Bunny."

"Demetrius, don't."

It was her turn to stare into his eyes, her blue-green set blazing with determination even through the film that her medication cast. Demetrius opened his mouth and then closed it. He relented.

"Let me draw you a bath," He kissed her forehead and then disappeared into the bathroom. Bunny sat on the bed and laid back, hair surrounding her like a halo. It felt like a smudge now. Her mother had sworn repeatedly that she'd find the document and have it waiting for her. It was foolish to have believed her.

She just didn't realize things would go as sideways as they did. Bunny was expecting there to be some screaming, door slamming, and maybe even a few things thrown. She didn't think it would get quite that physical.

There was a certain satisfaction felt in seeing Demetrius clock her father. In fact, if it weren't for the mixture of emotions, she'd be practically giddy about it. She'd longed to do the same thing for so many years but just wasn't strong enough to get away with it. She sighed, taking a deep breath. Of course, the big, strong man had come in to rescue her. But he was pretty hot and made her wildest dreams come true. So, he could stay.

When Demetrius came back, he scooped her up and brought her to the tub. Candles were lit all around, painting flickering shadows across the walls and floor. A rich, sweet aroma was thick in the air. He had also poured champagne into glass flutes and placed a platter of chocolate-covered strawberries sitting on a standing tray.

"Where did you get all of this?" She asked, looking around in confusion. They hadn't stopped anywhere except for his apartment.

"Oh, I called ahead and had everything set up for when we arrived," Demetrius answered as though that had been plainly obvious, his hand testing the water temperature. He was picky about it, having learned her preferences. She decided not to question it further. Bunny stripped out of her clothing without the normal flair she used to catch his eye. For once, she wasn't in the mood to have sex with him.

Demetrius seemed to get the message. He kissed her forehead and said he had some work to finish up for a class, and that she should take her time.

He didn't have to tell her twice.

Chapter 26

Bunny soaked for what must have been at least an hour. Normally, she'd want a good book or a show to keep her company. Today, she wanted to reflect on everything that had happened. She wondered when he would buckle under the pressure. They always did. Her mind was broken from what she had seen, what had been done. Bunny wasn't afraid of that truth.

It had ruined her life enough times that she couldn't be afraid, only numb to the things she did to fulfill the prophecy hovering above her head like the blade of a guillotine. Something inside of Bunny screamed with an intensity that shook her when she got too close to another human being. It was unsafe. It would end in misery. It had to stop on her terms.

She was drinking the champagne like true-bred trailer trash, guzzling instead of sipping. Bunny wasn't in a "sip and savor" sort of mood. She wanted the burn of alcohol in her veins. It was the strength she needed to do what had to be done.

Chocolate was smeared across her fingers. He knew chocolate-covered fruit was a weakness of hers. Bunny had a bit of a sweet tooth and the fruit made her feel like it was healthier. When she had explained this to Demetrius, he had laughed at her. "Sure, honey Bunny," He'd crooned indulgently, stroking her hair.

Since then, she'd been greeted by a few different couriers carrying chocolate-covered fruit platters. The worst of it had been in a couple of classes before she'd made their relationship public. She'd chased him down the second time it happened and pegged chocolate-covered grapes at him in front of everybody on their campus' cafe patio. Later that night, he had pulled the car over and dragged her into the backseat.

There, on the side of a very public road, he spanked her heavily for wasting the food. Then, he'd grabbed her hair and pulled her head back so her ear was by his mouth, her back arched painfully.

"You were asking for the attention, Bunny. Practically begging for it. If you don't make it clear that you belong to me, I sure as hell will." Bunny shuddered from the memory, lowering herself deeper into the steaming water to prevent the frigid shiver from building at the base of her spine.

The champagne was seeping into her system, blurring the edges of her emotions until they all bled into one amalgamation of feeling. It was anger. Bunny was pissed. She was mad about how she was raised, mad about how hard she had to struggle, mad about how she wanted so badly just to be loved and she couldn't–

A gasping sob escaped her mouth at the thought, one that slipped through the cracks even as she wasn't trying to dig quite that deep.

She turned to the breathing exercises her therapist had taught her: in through the mouth, out through the nose. Slow, steady, measured. It began working and her head stopped spinning. The water was starting to make her dizzy, however, and she decided it was time to go out and face the finality waiting for her in the other room.

Wrapped in a fluffy towel, Bunny stepped out of the balmy bathroom and into the crisp air provided by the rest of the suite. Demetrius was standing in the living area, a glass of champagne in hand, watching the water through the windows.

"We need to talk."

He turned at the sound of her voice, eyebrows raised and eyes widening. Demetrius set the flute down on the coffee table and made his way toward her.

"What's up, honey Bunny?" He asked, tone gentle but edged with a nervous vein.

"I don't think this is working out."

"No," His voice was soft but had a tone of finality.

"Excuse me?" Bunny replied, confused.

"Bunny, we're not doing this. You're upset, you're scared, and you're trying to protect yourself the only way you know how," He sighed before continuing, "You want to leave before you can be left, especially now that you're really feeling for the other person and you have something to lose."

"You have no idea-"

"Don't interrupt me, Bunny. I do have an idea. I absolutely do. You have such an incredible need to control everything around you. That's what this is— that's what we are."

"What do you mean?" Bunny's voice was feather light.

"I mean that you need to learn how to let control go, Bunny, and I need to learn how to take it. That's why we do what we do."

"Demetrius, you're the most in control-" She began, laughing softly and shaking her head. He cut her off quickly.

"No, that's who I want you to see, Bunny. That's a carefully curated image. But I'm scared, y'know? I'm scared all the time. I'm filled with doubt about every decision I have to make," He took a step toward her, "Except for when it comes to you."

Bunny took a step back, unsure where this was going but not entirely sure she liked it. He continued to talk, undeterred by her body language.

"I don't talk about it a lot, but my OCD rules my life, baby. Even on medication, even in therapy. And it made me scared of doing anything for a really long time. When I saw you at that party, I had never wanted to bring a woman to heel more in my life. Your neck was begging for my collar. For a few moments, I knew for certain what I wanted to do."

He stopped, looking unsure of himself. Bunny was frozen in place, holding her breath as she listened to his confession. This felt important, like exactly what she had been waiting for without realizing it.

"It was the first time in a long time I've made a decision so earnestly and easily, my love." Demetrius had begun edging his way toward her, Bunny still in the same position, clutching her bath towel to her chest. She allowed him to get within a foot of her before whispering, "Fire hydrant."

He stopped immediately.

There was silence, but it was heavy. Bunny swore she could hear the drops of water slowly falling from her hair to the floor. Time felt as though it had stopped, a vastness stretching between them as the safe word hung in the middle, an impermeable boundary he wouldn't dream of defying.

"Bunny, we don't… have to do anything," Demetrius said, head cocking to the side as he regarded her with a curious eye.

"I just want to make it clear that I don't want you to hurt me tonight. You've hurt me enough already." Demetrius sucked a breath in through his teeth. Images of her father, blood pouring through his fingers, came back to her. He had only been protecting her. Even so, watching her parent being victimized by violence was difficult.

"You've hurt me, too, Bunny," He said finally, eyes tracing slow lines across everything in the room to avoid meeting hers. It was her turn to move forward. Bunny had still been clutching the fluffy towel, but now she let it drop as she moved her arms to wrap around his waist. Her body suctioned to his, the wetness seeping into his clothing.

Demetrius tensed.

"I'm sorry," She whispered into his chest. It felt like something inside of her was being exposed to him again. There was so much she could apologize for. If there was one thing she knew, it was that she was a hard person to love.

He sighed into her hair and said, "Bunny,

let's go to bed. I'm tired." She agreed with him immediately and he scooped her up, walking into the bedroom.

Chapter 27

Demetrius laid her down gently on the king-sized bed before stripping off his damp shirt. Next came the pants, and boxer briefs. Bunny was wrapped up in the soft duvet, stealing glances out of the corner of her eye.

Once he was ready, Demetrius climbed into bed next to her. Bunny squeaked when he wrapped his arms around her, pulling her close. He kissed her on the side of her head, her earlobe, her pulse point.

She let loose a low moan when he pressed his lips to her neck again and lingered there. She had used her safe word, but consent could be given back so long as she wasn't being pressured. He had explained that to her previously. She turned around so that their naked torsos were pressed together. His eyes were dark and moody, and she could feel his iron-like manhood pressing into her belly. Demetrius leaned his head down.

"Bunny, baby, are you sure you want this?" She pressed her face into his neck, breathing in deeply, "Demetrius, I need you so badly. I just don't want to hurt anymore today."

With that, he somehow managed to pull her even closer, wrapping his arms around her back.

"I don't hurt you, Bunny. I free you." Before she could respond, his lips were on hers, tongue searching gently for entry she quickly gave. He was flavored with champagne and she moaned into his mouth. Her head was swimming with the same taste.

He shifted his weight and moved her in the process so that she was on her back and he was leaning over her. Demetrius' leg ended up between her own and she instinctively ground her core into him. The responding growl made her squeal in glee.

"What was that noise?" He laughed into her neck, kissing gently as one of his hands began exploring the curves of her body.

Bunny didn't get a chance to respond

beyond giggling sweetly. There was something about him that made her feel bright and innocent. It meant little, girlish laughs bubbled out even while he was gearing up to fuck her mercilessly.

His mouth settled over one of her breasts, tongue swirling around the pebbled peak. Bunny gasped and bucked her hips. Her swollen lips were plump with desire and whispered moans slipped from between them as he pleasured her.

"God, Bunny, you're so fucking wet," He groaned, his hand gliding between her legs, a finger trailing up her dripping core. He leaned close to her before whispering, "You don't ask to come tonight, Bunny. Your pleasure is yours to take as much or as little as you'd like, baby. Just tell me what you want."

She whimpered loudly when he began positioning his head between her legs. His warm breath sighed out against her pussy, making her head swim with desire. Demetrius kissed her thighs, slowly trailing down toward her center, taking his time.

"Demetrius," She cried out, wincing at the sound of her own voice; it resonated with the desperation that she was drowning in. Without further fuss, a warm tongue slipped between her folds and began toying with her clit. Bunny gasped and her hips shook. Her hands flew down to tangle in his hair, pulling gently when he hit a particularly good place.

Demetrius brought two fingers to her entrance, sliding them in gently, curling once he was inside of her up to his first knuckles. The feeling of his moving fingers combined with that warm, wet tongue on her clit sent Bunny over the edge.

She screamed as she shattered, her thighs crushing together with his head between them. He made no move to stop her. Instead, Demetrius kept licking, sucking, curling, and kissing while she came. He knew exactly what she wanted, and that was to keep the orgasm going as long as possible. Finally, her body jerking and words indecipherable, she started pushing his head away. Immediately, Demetrius pulled up, his eyes bright with concern. She smiled gently, heart warming as she realized in that moment how much he cared.

"My turn," She said, "Get on your back."

He grinned in response, moving out from between her legs and up the bed until he was resting against the headboard. It was a demand he was not about to deny. Bunny crawled up to him, admiring the shape of his rock-hard cock. His thick shaft had a slight curve in it so that it pointed toward him, the head bulbous and purple.

When she was between his legs, she got on all fours and bent down to run her tongue from base to tip. She knew he'd love watching the curve of her ass bob in the air as she blew him. The immense stature of his manhood always gave her pause, but she was excited to hear how he'd come undone when she used her mouth. Bunny positioned herself, opened her throat by tensing her neck, and took the entire length in one go. Demetrius groaned, twisting the sheets in his clawing hands. He was already losing his mind.

The salty taste of precum filled her mouth and she bobbed, sucking in as she pulled back up. She realized that he was whimpering her name, and that was all the encouragement she needed. Bunny began using every trick she knew, moaning as she worked him into a frenzy, pussy pulsing with the knowledge that this man was losing his mind because of what she was doing to him.

And then, a hand around her throat, gently pushing her back.

"God- fuck, Bunny, stop," He groaned, panting heavily as sweat beaded his forehead. His dark hair was plastered there in little spikes. He looked like a mess. She loved it.

Bunny pouted and watched him as he steadied his breathing. She wanted to feel him come down her throat, and tonight was supposed to be about her.

Demetrius glanced up and noticed. He began laughing before reaching out and pulling her close to him using a hand around the back of her neck. Once she was snuggled into his chest, he whispered, "Bunny, I want to make love to you tonight. I can fuck your face until I come down your throat later."

With that, they kissed deeply, and she felt herself melting into him. He was being risky, using a term like love, but Bunny felt so warm and safe that she allowed herself to relish in it instead of being repulsed.

Somebody wanted to make love to her. He picked her up as he rose to his knees and then flipped them over, Bunny landing softly on her back with their limbs tangled. She giggled in delight as he brushed soft kisses on her neck, scrunching her shoulder in as his lips tickled the sensitive skin. Demetrius held himself over her just slightly, using his forearms to brace his weight. They stared into each other's eyes for a few moments and Bunny could feel something break inside of her.

"Bunny?"

"Yeah?"

Instead of responding, he leaned down and caught her lips. She returned the kiss in earnest, wrapping her arms around his neck and grinding her core onto his cock. It slowed until they were languidly brushing their lips, his hand reaching down. He positioned himself and, with a sigh, slid himself into her up to the hilt. Bunny cried out softly, head falling back and eyes squeezing shut.

Demetrius was just so big.

He began moving his hips slowly, dragging in and out of her with loud groans that made it sound like his world was shattering. Her world was falling apart all around her, too. Bunny panted and writhed underneath him. This was so different from how they usually had sex. There were no rules, no expectations, no punishments.

Just his hot body suctioned to hers, their lips softly searching for purchase on slick skin.

"Oh, God, Bunny, you feel so good," He moaned into her ear, picking up the pace but keeping the rhythm that had her pulsing with pleasure, as though she were a levy, waves splashing so far up they sprayed out over the top. The dam was about to break. His hand found hers and Demetrius curled his fingers through hers, holding her hand softly but firmly. She knew he was close when he began chanting her name into the air. She was close, too.

"Come with me, baby," She cried out, wrapping her legs around his waist and grinding herself into him, seeking pressure on her clit. Demetrius responded by reaching a hand between them, albeit awkwardly. His fingers found what they were searching out, however, and Bunny howled as the pleasure surged.

Within seconds, she was flying over the edge, her mouth locked on his as he began to pump into her at a punishing speed. After a few seconds, they both collapsed, their chests heaving and bodies covered in a sheen of sweat.

He rolled off of her, still panting from the effort. Not knowing what else to do, Bunny stuck a hand out. Demetrius eyed it, before looking to her with a questioning look on his face.

"High five?" She offered weakly.

Demetrius immediately started laughing. He weakly high-fived her, rolled onto his side, grabbed her face gently, and kissed her again.

"You are the most incredible person I have ever met, Bunny," He murmured, brushing his fingers across her face.

"I'm sorry about your luck with people."

"Bunny, I'm being serious."

"So am I."

They both laughed, settling into each other's arms, and drifted off.

Chapter 28

The next morning, she could smell breakfast before she could see it, mostly because she was trying her best not to open her eyes. She knew he would have gotten a sampling of everything on the menu. Bunny didn't have to look to confirm that. This was for two reasons: the first, because breakfast was her favorite meal and he'd want all of her favorites present, and the second, she wasn't awake to confirm what she did or didn't want.

"Good morning, good morning," A singsong voice dripping in sunshine spoke softly next to her ear. Bunny groaned, pushing his face away.

"Come on, honey Bunny. We have a long day ahead of us, so you need to get up and eat." She was going to put up more of a struggle until he purred into her ear that he didn't mind starting his day with her over his knee. Bunny gasped, shoving him gently, but got out of bed finally. Curiosity was eating away at her, but she wasn't going to ask about their big day. She had too much on her mind for this early in the morning.

Bunny joined Demetrius at the long table next to the kitchenette in the suite. He had laid out everything and it looked incredible. There were pancakes, crepes, toppings for both, scrambled eggs, bacon, sausage, oatmeal… The list went on.

As had become customary, Demetrius made her plate while she sat like a princess. Even if the concept was revolting to her initially, she knew it was something she could see herself getting used to. It no longer felt like a man doing something simple for her as though she couldn't herself.

No, now it felt like somebody cared about her so deeply that they would serve her in any capacity possible, even literally so. Bunny loved that he was so devoted to her in every aspect, and it extended far beyond the bedroom.

Demetrius' control was all-encompassing.

She was absolutely drunk off of the power that came with his ownership. While he may hold the leash, she held him in the palm of her hand. It was never about him. Instead, every scene, every depraved sexual encounter, was imagined and formed by Bunny herself.

Once her plate was made, Demetrius began serving himself. She waited patiently until he was done before eating from her own. At first, he had tried to rush her along, insisting she eat immediately. That was the one place she dug her heels in, however. She wouldn't eat before he did. Eventually, he relented, and Bunny could wait patiently for him in peace.

Breakfast was quiet. While they had worked out a good bit of tension between the sheets, there were still things to be discussed. Bunny wasn't ready to bring up her parents, and he wasn't ready to apologize for decking her father in the face. Granted, she wasn't sure he ever would be.

The crepes were her favorite part. She ate three; one with Nutella and strawberries, one withpeach jam, and the last with baked apple slices. She was also a fan of the eggs and made quick work of them. Both sausage and bacon were present, as well. Bunny had always enjoyed a big, hearty breakfast. She worked at a barn, so she needed the fuel to get through her days.

"Are you ready for an adventure?" Demetrius asked, looking at her from over the rim of his coffee cup. Bunny cocked her head to the side, staring at him expectantly.

"It's a surprise, honey Bunny. You're going to love it."

She pouted in the face of the unknown but said nothing in response. Demetrius told her to get ready for the day and to bring a coat since they'd be outside around half the time. She wasn't sure what that meant, but a part of her was cautiously excited.

The downtown area was charming. White lights twinkled overhead, criss-crossed on the lampposts so they provided a lattice ceiling. All the buildings were red brick and attached. Bunny thought it looked like something out of a movie-some hidden, peaceful place only accessible through a silver screen. There were tasteful decorations everywhere you looked, signaling the turn of seasons and the arrival of the holiday season.

Bunny had forgotten it was approaching so quickly. She hadn't even thought about what to get Demetrius. Or, if he even celebrated. Somehow it hadn't come up. They had spoken about everything under the sun, but it was almost always philosophical. They never ventured into personal territory, mostly due to her hesitancy in the face of that type of intimacy. Demetrius toed the line but respected her boundaries when push came to shove.

"Do you celebrate?" She asked, looking up at him. She was hanging onto his arm, which was crooked at the elbow.

"I'm sorry?" He asked, glancing at her.

"Christmas. Do you celebrate it?"

"I mean, we do, yes. Why?"

"I don't know. I just realized I had no idea."

"Do you?"

"No."

She said it with such a finality that Demetrius knew better than to push. Bunny wasn't even sure why she said she didn't– she had plenty of times in the past. But somehow, this year felt different. Bunny was certain he'd have some extravagant offering, and she couldn't come close to matching that. It would feel unequal, as most things between them did at one point or another.

Beyond that, Christmas had terrible memories attached to it. She wasn't in a rush to revisit the past. It was just too painful for her, especially when she was still licking her wounds regarding many of the people involved.

Her parents, for example.

There wasn't a chance in hell that she would tell any of this to Demetrius. She didn't want him to know. He would be far too quick to try and fix the situation by providing what he perceived to be the best memory possible. It would overwhelm her. It would be far too much, and it would scare her, and she would react poorly. She always did when she was frightened.

They held hands as they meandered down the path in the park at the center of town. She loved the way the sky above them was filtered through a brilliant web of light, and that the crisp night air felt cooling on her cheeks, which were pink with heat.

"Let's go inside somewhere?" She

pleaded, putting her other hand on his arm. Bunny was peering at him with what she knew was an expression he could never argue with; she was pleading like a child. She swore sometimes that it felt like he was trying to make up for her childhood. Bunny wasn't sure if she loved or hated that. He wanted her to have all the experiences she had been denied. Most importantly, she thought that perhaps he wanted her to feel the love that she had been owed but never had.

Bunny could feel how intensely he felt about her. It had become something she lived in awe of. It felt bright enough to block out the sun; sometimes it hurt to look at him for the adoration that shone from his eyes.

Demetrius was scanning, but it seemed that he had found a worthy target. He began walking, guiding her down a long path to a crosswalk. Bunny didn't take notice of where they were going. She preferred to just be led by him. It took all the pressure away from her. For once, she could relinquish control entirely.

It ended up that they were heading into an antique store. It was filled to the brim with knicknacks shoved into the nooks and crannies of towering furniture. All of it was handmade, and all of it was delightfully crafted. Bunny immediately felt herself brighten. Demetrius made her take off her coat, slinging it over his arm before she was allowed to wander. She walked slowly, running her fingers over an item now and again if it caught her attention.

He knew how much she loved old things. It extended far beyond her degree– Bunny was also a frequent antiquer. She loved finding little treasures hidden among the mess often accompanying these stores. It was almost like being at an archaeological dig. Her breath caught in her throat when she spotted two gorgeous horse head bookends. She immediately gravitated toward them, touching them gently, before turning over the price tag.

Once more, her breath caught in her throat.

They were $500.

She shot a look at Demetrius, who was looking at some books in a different corner. Then she remembered that this was a bougie part of town. It would stand to reason that the antique store would reflect the prices the wealthy were primed to pay. With a sigh, Bunny turned and almost ran directly into Demetrius. She gasped, and he laughed softly at her, before reaching a hand out to cup her face.

"Relax, baby, it's okay," He kissed her forehead and Bunny smiled softly.

"Find something you like?" He asked, peering over her shoulder. He was bound to have spotted the set she was intently studying just a few moments ago.

"Yes, but they're way out of my price range. Let's go," She said the first part quickly and then prodded him. Demetrius was undeterred.

"If you want the bookends, Bunny, they're yours," His voice was gentle, pleading, begging her to just accept his gesture.

"Demetrius, I don't want the bookends. I mean that. I don't."

"But if they were to somehow end up in your dorm…"

"Fire hydrant."

He started at that, looking at her curiously. She whispered it on a breath, but with all the sternness she could muster. Demetrius regarded Bunny for a moment before he smiled softly, pulled her closer, and said, "Loud and clear, honey Bunny."

Chapter 29

When it came to food, she allowed him to spoil her relentlessly. Bunny could be swayed with a good meal in even the worst of times. A bad mood could usually be countered with carbs.

They sat in a little restaurant she was sure reservations were required to get into. She felt woefully underdressed for the occasion, but Demetrius seemed comfortable even in his casual wear. She tried to emulate his confidence. They ordered escargot, bacon-wrapped scallops, and a host of other goodies for their appetizers. She loved having leftovers.

Normally, by the end of the night, she'd eat them drunk on the kitchen floor. Demetrius had once said it was the most beautiful thing he had ever seen. She told him to stop romanticizing her messiest moments.

Her margarita was perfectly prepared, and it was absolutely potent. She felt herself drawn to sipping from it perhaps too often. Soon, the effects of alcohol were starting to take hold. The restaurant seemed that much glitzier when the lights were smudged in her blurring vision. There was a gorgeous chandelier in the center of the room, and under it were round tables with brilliantly white tablecloths.

Everything was adorned in gold and brocade patterns alongside natural oak. It was dimly lit, and there was a whisper of smoke in the air from the candles placed on every table. Bunny was gazing dreamily at her surroundings until Demetrius reached over.

He took one of her hands, rubbing his thumb over the top of one. They locked eyes and stayed there, entranced. It was an irresistible pull they both felt. No matter how far they wandered, they were destined to find each other again.

"Bunny?"

"Yes?"

"You need to slow down on the margaritas."

She gaped at him, looking equal parts startled

and offended.

"Okay, fine," She said, extending the second word in a defeated tone. Bunny pushed the margarita away and instead reached for the goblet of water that had been served alongside it. Bunny sipped thoughtfully, excited for the filets to arrive. She wanted nothing more than to carve into a steak that would turn to butter in her mouth. The current offerings were more than enough to assure her that the rest of the food would be incredible.

"So, Bunny, what are your holiday season plans?" He sounded hesitant, tiptoeing around the real issue. Despite what she had said previously, she normally had plans, and she wasn't sure how to reconcile that with his desire to have her with him. Bunny spent almost every holiday with Brianna, who didn't have family nearby and didn't like them all that much, either.

"I'm not sure," She said, piercing a scallop with her fork. She lifted it to her mouth and savored every bit of the bite. It was tender and succulent. The bacon added a wonderful layer of crunch and a sweet-salty aftertaste that left her craving more.

She might ask for an order to take home.

Sometimes she'd do that, shyly asking the waiter if he could pack her up one to go. Demetrius always smiled like he was proud of her for asking at all.

"I might be with Brianna. I don't like leaving her alone on holidays…" She trailed off, feeling a pang of guilt at even the thought. It was their tradition and she hated breaking it.

She hadn't really been talking about the holiday itself when she said she didn't celebrate. No, she and Brianna always made a big dinner and then played board games long into the night over drinks. What she didn't do was buy into the commercialism that drove the holiday season. Neither Bunny nor Brianna exchanged gifts of any kind. Instead, they'd focus their money on coming up with the ingredients for a feast and carrying it out.

"What if you and Brianna came to my parent's house?" He asked, sounding hopeful. She groaned inwardly at realizing he had known all along what her plans were. How, she wasn't sure, but it was likely an obvious choice for her.

Bunny paused, considering it.

"Well, I can ask her."

"Please do. It would mean the world to my

parents if you'd join us."

Bunny pursed her lips. He knew it was a soft point of hers. She loved his parents and the guilt of disappointing them would kill her. It was almost assured that she would be present.

Manipulative bastard, she thought to herself.

When the main course showed up, they both tucked in happily. Afterward, they declined dessert, drained their drinks, and walked out with their leftovers. The night wasn't over, however. Demetrius had told her to leave room for something sweet afterward, just not at that restaurant. He was holding the food in one hand, his arm crooked so that she could slide her own through it. They walked down the busy sidewalk, moving with the speed of the crowd. Bunny was buzzing with excitement, and it was all Demetrius could do to keep her from bouncing off.

She had most certainly had a little too much to drink with dinner. It had been a while since she felt glee like this that wasn't the product of a pill or powder. Demetrius had a surprise and she wanted to know what it was. It was just simple, and pure. She had never liked surprises before, but he always seemed to be perfectly in line with her desires.

Finally, they walked up to a stand that was serving apple crisp with ice cream, and hot cider. Bunny could have squealed with excitement. Those were two of her favorite things to eat in the cold season.

They got into line and, when it was their turn, Bunny was all too excited to order. But, looking at Demetrius, she realized she would prefer to just defer. She listened to him relay what he knew she wanted, and they waited over by the pick-up window.

When their order finally arrived, Bunny wasted no time in taking a bite. It was perfection; creamy soft serve first, and then the softness of apples and the crunch of the topping. If there was a heaven, she was sure this dessert would be on the menu every day. Demetrius was slowly eating his own, staring at her as they stood under a streetlight, huddled together. Bunny felt the pressure of his eyes. She shifted uncomfortably under the weight.

"Demetrius?"

"Yeah, Bunny?"

"Let's go back soon."

"Anything you want, baby."

The exchange was given around

mouthfuls, both of them happily munching under the soft light above. The air was soothing and smelt almost like snow, a promise of what was to come. She was nestled in a form-fitting beige sweater with a dark green vest layered on top. Her blue jeans fell straight around a pair of duck boots.

He had on his favorite black peacoat, and a thin scarf tossed around his neck. Bunny thought he looked exquisite, his facial structure lending shadows in the light that made him appear brooding, haunting.

It made her heart beat a little faster.

Chapter 30

Once they were back, Demetrius placed the leftovers in the fridge and pulled out a bottle of champagne. When Bunny wrinkled her nose, he pulled out a bottle of orange juice. She perked up immediately.

"How about some music?" He said as he filled two glass flutes. Bunny agreed noncommittally, caught up in stripping out of her clothing so she could get into something more comfortable. She slipped into the bedroom to get her pajamas. When she came back, he had Franz Ferdinand playing from a Bluetooth speaker on the coffee table. She rolled her eyes, and her thin, soft shirt ran up her stomach as she crossed her arms.

"What? You did this to yourself,"

Demetrius said, grinning.

"I was joking when I said it was your only personality trait."

"And somehow still correct. You're so perceptive, Bunny."

She groaned but caught herself smiling widely. The wood was glassy under her slippers, which she stayed tucked into most of the time she lounged indoors in the winter.

They stood in the kitchenette, sipping champagne in the warm silence that stretched on. It was often they would do this, enjoying the company of the other without having to fill the space between them with noise. Eventually, though, one of them would always end up ending the cozy moment. The other wasn't often left complaining. Bunny looked up at Demetrius when he put his empty glass down, eyeing her in a way she felt was deeply suspicious.

"Bunny, do you dance?"

"Absolutely not."

"Wrong answer."

She had only seconds to prepare for him to scoop her up in a bridal-style hold. Bunny squeaked, wrapping her arms around his neck. He walked them into the living room and started spinning her around.

"See? We're dancing!"

"Put me down!"

Even while she protested, a tinkling laughter escaped her and she delighted in his attention. Finally, he placed her on her feet, but immediately took her hands and started making movements she thought were reminiscent of an ostrich flinging its wings around during a mating dance.

"Demetrius, come on…" She started, backing away. He paid no heed to her complaints and continued twisting his hips and trying to lure her into whatever horrible movement he was showing off now.

"Bunny, you come on! It's fun!" His smile was so infectious that she felt herself grinning in response.

And then, she let go.

Bunny twirled into his arms. They danced together, Demetrius dipping her low at times, spinning her like a top at others. It was sloppy and silly, and there was an undeniable warmth in her belly that had nothing to do with sex. Franz Ferdinand was still playing faithfully in the background. Demetrius pulled her back to his chest and held her there, burying his face in her neck and singing the lyrics of the chorus to her.

Bunny was shrieking with delight at this point, far beyond the point of shame or holding herself back. They fed off of each other's energy, giggling in an endless cycle that had them collapsing to the floor in a mess of limbs and laughs.

"Bunny?"

"Yeah, Demetrius?"

Their faces were inches away from each other, and she was surrounded by cedar and smoke. He paused, wetting his lips, looking hesitant, before finally speaking.

"I think I want to do this for the rest of my life."

She stilled, face frozen in a now too-wide smile. Her heart told her to confirm his words, to tell him that she desperately wanted nothing more. But something inside her said that this was a dangerous game.

"Hey, hey, hey," He said, propping up on an elbow and reaching his hand out to hold her cheek. Bunny shook away his hand, sitting up.

"Bunny, baby, what's wrong?" He pleaded. She wasn't meeting his face, instead blushing in the other direction as she realized she'd ruined what could have been a beautiful moment between them.

"It's nothing, I'm just tired," She offered weakly, fidgeting with her hands.

"Why don't we head to bed, baby?"

Bunny finally looked at him and smiled, nodding her head in agreement. He helped her up and then walked over to the speaker, turning it off. Her body began to warm at the idea of sliding between the covers with him. She followed him obediently as he started toward the bedroom. He was already sliding his shirt from his body, back muscles flexing in a way that made her mouth water.

Demetrius stood in front of the bed, and Bunny joined him, molding herself to his chest. He held her tight, rocking back and forth, before he finally asked, "What do you want tonight? Do you need me to love or free you?"

She trembled in his arms, not from fear or cold, but from incredible anticipation she felt. Naturally, the only response she could give was, "I want you to be enough of a man to make a decision by yourself."

Bunny felt Demetrius suck in a breath.

"Oh, so that's how you want it."

Chapter 31

Within seconds, the chase was on. She spun around and leaped away from him, but he was on her in an instant. They fell to the floor and Demetrius immediately made his way into a seated position, struggling to drape her over his lap.

Finally, he grabbed a fistful of her hair and yanked her head back, his mouth to her ear. Bunny gasped for air, she felt hot and melted further when she registered his words.

"Bunny, I'm warning you right now that I have all night and a lot of patience. Behave yourself or we can find out how many orgasms it takes before that pretty pussy squirts for me."

She opened her mouth, ready to be offended by his language, but the fire in her belly had risen to a roaring inferno. A part of her had to wonder how much it would take to make that happen. While she was paused in thought, Demetrius took the opportunity to spin her around so that she was in position. He slowly pulled her pajama shorts over her ass, letting them bunch at the top of her thighs.

He wrapped his hand around her throat and pulled back so her back was arched. Demetrius kissed her temple before whispering, "I want you to play with yourself the entire time, Bunny. I want you nice and wet when I'm done."

Bunny swallowed heavily before slipping a hand between her legs. It was an awkward position, but with a little perseverance, she could make it work. She would make it work if only to please him.

A little moan escaped her as her fingers found what they were searching for. She whimpered and bucked her hips gently.

"Don't come, baby," He reminded her gently, before rubbing her ass with his hand. Bunny was already fighting the stirrings of her climax.

His hand came up and landed with a heavy sound. She yelped but diligently rubbed and stroked her aching clit. This continued for a few more blows until Bunny was whimpering and shivering.

Demetrius lifted her off his lap and stood up. She lay on the floor, panting slightly, while he rooted around in a black duffel bag containing the toys they'd brought. He pulled out a butt plug, a vibrator, and a strange vibrator, along with cuffs and ropes.

She nearly blanched, feeling her stomach tighten. She wasn't sure what he had planned, but it was looking like his sadistic side was on display.

"Bunny, get on the bed," He crooned, walking to the bathroom for what she assumed would be a couple of towels. She did as she was told, climbing onto the tall king-sized bed.

Once she was nestled into the duvet, Bunny watched for Demetrius, who shortly returned. He was carrying two towels. She held her breath as he approached; he was surrounded by a bright silhouette from the bathroom light. It made him look positively heavenly… Which was too bad. She knew him for the devil he was. After what he had planned tonight, she was sure anybody would.

He laid a towel over the bed and pointed to it. He didn't need to speak. She crawled from under the covers, laying on her stomach across the towel where he had gestured.

"Take your clothing off for me, baby," He said, arms crossed lightly as he drank in the sight of her. Bunny quickly complied, putting on a little show for him as she peeled the shorts and tank top off. His breathing had become heavier, taking on a husky quality that made her core stir. She laid onto her stomach, laying her head on her crossed arms and looking at him expectantly.

Demetrius didn't break eye contact as he poured a generous amount of lube into his hand. He reached down, slipping between her ass cheeks and finding the tight entrance between them. He slipped in a finger, and then two, and Bunny finally looked away, squeezing her eyes shut as she whimpered. He twisted and scissored his fingers until he thought she was ready, and then positioned the plug.

Bunny mewled pathetically in response, pressing her hips back so she was pressing into the toy. Demetrius had coated it in lube, as well, and the slick silicone quickly slid inside of her, Bunny gasping as the entrance snapped shut around the plug's stem. It was weighty and large. She could feel the toy inside of her, especially as she wriggled and flexed and tried to get used to the sensation.

Demetrius wiped himself off, and then wiped her down, as well. She moaned in appreciation of the plush cotton rubbing against her heated skin. He threw the fluffy, white towel to the floor once he was done.

"On your back, Bunny. Spread eagle."

His command was said in that low, dark tone that made her feel desire bubbling between her legs. She complied, spreading her arms and legs out, breathing heavily. She felt him secure cuffs around each extremity and then was pulled tight one limb at a time.

When he was done, Bunny could hardly move anything. She wiggled, testing her restraints, and found herself tightly bound. Her breathing became quicker, more shallow, the plug still heavy inside of her. The bed dipped and her head whipped toward the disturbance.

Demetrius had the other toys in hand, and Bunny's belly flipped at the thought of him using them on her. One was a long stem with a bulbous end that was angled slightly. The other was her favorite clitoral stimulator. She whimpered pathetically and pushed her face into her shoulder when he settled beside her, propped up on his side by his arm. Demetrius angled his head down so he could kiss her gently.

"You've been so horribly behaved tonight, Bunny," He said softly to her, "But that's okay. You couldn't have gotten yourself out of this even if you had been on your best behavior."

Here, he leaned in, holding her face and pulling it closer to his. Bunny could feel warm breath brush across her plump lips.

"I've wanted to do this to you for so long. Nothing could have stopped me from finally seeing you this vulnerable."

It was true. She was entirely bared to him, unable to resist, and panic crept in around the edges when she considered these things. But then she'd look at him, and all of the doubt melted away. Bunny trusted Demetrius in an almost inexplicable way. His presence provided comfort that soothed her in even the most erotic situations he guided her through.

Demetrius reached out and smoothed the hair over her forehead. "Relax, Bunny," He crooned, leaning in to nuzzle her neck, "Just let go, baby. I'm here. It's okay."

With that, he pulled away from her and she sucked in sharply. The buzz of the vibrator signaled the beginning of what she was sure was going to be the longest night of her life. The toy was soon positioned perfectly over her clit, the seal suctioning the sucking mechanism over her swollen bud. Bunny whined and writhed, already feeling a burgeoning orgasm building quickly in her belly.

She began moaning, pleading with him to stop, her hips bucking wildly even despite the restraints. Bunny gasped and choked on her breath as the first orgasm finally rolled over her.

The fire was fanning out between her legs, especially as he began tapping the vibrator up and down. The new sensation drove her over the edge into another climax, this one pounding unforgivingly through her body as she cried out for mercy. Bunny was breathing rapidly, her entire body taut as she pulled against what was holding her.

In an instant, the vibrator was gone, and Demetrius was kissing her.

"You're doing so good for me, Bunny," He purred, "Take a break for a little while, okay?"

Chapter 32

Bunny could feel the sizeable plug in her ass. Every time she came, it felt like she was being fucked with the toy for how hard she tensed and released with the power of her climax. Sweat collected all over, beading across her body as she struggled to bring her breathing under control, small shockwaves punishing her throbbing pussy. She tried not to think about the fact that he was far from done.

Demetrius returned what seemed like only seconds later. She hadn't even realized he had gotten off the bed. He climbed back into position next to her, stroking her cheek with a finger as she panted pathetically.

"I think you want a little more, my greedy girl," His tone was dripping with honey, the sweetness sticky and leaving her feeling dirtier than ever. Bunny mewled pathetically, letting out sounds of protest as he gently slipped a hand between her legs.

There was also a bottle of lube, and Demetrius began pouring a generous amount on the vibrator he had brought with him. She felt like passing out. He had told her at one point that lube was non-negotiable in most situations because it made everything feel better. "The wetter, the better," He had sang to her, laughing heartily. Strangely enough, he was correct.

Right now, she wished he wasn't, because she didn't need anything to feel more intense than it already did.

Demetrius slowly dragged the vibrator up and down her slit before positioning it at the entrance. Bunny wasn't sure how much more she could take, and he was adding something new to the mix.

She shifted again, muscles straining slightly against her bonds. The pleasant buzz was back and she could feel a molten seed of desire take root, primed to flourish in the fertile space deep in her belly.

Something was inherently hot to her

about him doing this. Demetrius gained nothing except mental satisfaction from these encounters. His focus was simply on making her feel things she never thought possible. She had never known him to be dissuaded from this calling. He wasn't getting his dick wet, yet was still somehow more than happy to spend his nights making her come until she cried. It clicked for her, just then.

He needs to learn how to take control, and I need to learn how to let it go... she thought to herself, his words echoing in her racing mind.

It all was gone in an instant, however, because Demetrius began sliding the vibrator in and out of her. The bulbous head dragged inside of her, angling up to hit every sweet spot along the way. It was an entirely new sensation, especially as the bulb began to buzz. She simultaneously wanted it all to end, and also for it to never stop.

Bunny's hips swayed from side to side, her eyes shut lightly, her head falling back so that her chin tipped to the ceiling. It was like being stuck in a trance. Finally, he had the toy lodged inside of her. Next, he spread her labia near the top to gain clear access to her clit again. She whimpered and tried to catch her breath. Bunny knew he would be merciless. He was on a mission.

The vibrator came down square on her throbbing bud, and she lifted off the bed with a scream. Bunny was whipping around as much as she could, desperate to get away from the horrible buzzing between her legs. It was too much. The pleasure bordered on pain as she quickly became overstimulated.

Between the vibrator in her pussy, the plug in her ass, and the suction on her clit, Bunny was quickly sinking in a ship she'd lost control of long ago. That was okay because, through the slits of her eyes, she could see her new captain. He would fish her out of the flotsam and she trusted that his vessel would carry her safely to whatever destination he saw fit.

Pressure built between her legs until her pussy fluttered in anticipation. Bunny was crying out shamelessly, begging for him to stop.

"I can't do this, please, Demetrius, no more," She half-sobbed, pressing her face into the sheets. Within seconds, she was crying out in pleasure again as another orgasm flooded her body.

Demetrius leaned down, his mouth next to her ear, "Yes, you can, Bunny."

She whined and mewled as he whispered gentle encouragement into her ear, the vibrator tapping up and down to pull yet more pleasure from her. Bunny was sure the duvet would be soaked with sweat now if it weren't for the towel; it was rolling off of her in waves.

He removed the clitoral vibrator and she gasped in relief, panting and thanking him between breaths. Bunny was certain she had never felt relief quite like this. Her entire body hurt from fighting the restraints, and she was certain at one point her orgasms had started coming so close together that the waves morphed into a single, flat line.

However, he came back to torture her more with a little squirt of lube. The lube allowed her vibrator to obtain a better seal, and the flicking mechanism that was punishing her clit slid deliciously over the bud. Bunny's throat was beginning to hurt.

And then relief came in the form of him taking away the vibrating toy once again. She lay there listless while desperately trying to hold onto consciousness. Demetrius smoothed the hair on her forehead, running the back of his pointer finger up and down her cheek after.

"Oh, poor Bunny," He crooned, "If you just gave me what I wanted, we could be done. But you're being stubborn, aren't you?"

She wanted to scream, to cry, to protest. Bunny hadn't ever squirted in her life. She had no idea how to make that happen, or if it was just something that just did. Of course, she could ask Demetrius… but that would ruin all the fun of finding out the hard way.

Bunny gasped in surprise and then let loose a throaty moan when she felt his warm tongue swirling around her nipple. She was back to wriggling pathetically and chanting his name. This only went on for a moment, however, because Demetrius had also brought over nipple clamps. Bunny protested weakly as he slid them into place and began to adjust them. He'd brushed a smidge of lube onto her peaks to lessen the pinch.

It was the little things for her.

Demetrius kissed her forehead and murmured, "Just a little more, baby, I promise. You can do this for me." She wanted to argue, to protest his assessment of her abilities, but Bunny was just too tired. At the sound of the vibrator, she felt dread clamp around her torso.

Bunny cried out as soon as he put the toy in place, screaming his name and begging him to stop.

"No, no, no, no," She chanted, head whipping from side to side. The stimulation was too much. It was too much. Bunny's entire body went taut, her sore muscles finding strength she didn't know was left to strain against what held her in place.

At the same time, Demetrius was rocking the toy lodged inside of her up and down, pressing the vibrating bulbous end into her g-spot in a way that made her go cross-eyed. After a brief struggle, she let the orgasm take her, eyes rolling to the back of her head. Bunny came until she was so sensitive it hurt, but still, she came more. The pain served to highlight the pleasure. It was an underscore to the pulsing in her pussy that made her whimper breathlessly.

Needing his reassurance, Bunny lifted her head to look at Demetrius. His eyes were like eclipsed moons- blackened, but there was an unmistakable light behind the darkness that soothed her.

Their eyes locked. Bunny opened her mouth, eyes widening, a new sensation flooding into her belly. This was different, as though she had ascended and found an entirely new plane of pleasure she hadn't realized existed. She knew it was possible to come until you almost blacked out; Demetrius had proved that theory more than once. But this new sensation was as if he had pushed her beyond that point, made her hold on until he could bring her to the next level.

Demetrius lay next to her on his side, body pressed to hers, face gently nuzzling into hers. He whispered gentle encouragement as she whimpered and wriggled.

"You're fine, Bunny. You can do this. Do you know how pretty you are when you're coming for me? So full you can hardly take it? I love watching you struggle to stay in control even as you're losing it so quickly. Keep coming undone for me, baby."

Bunny finally felt everything crash around her and then felt a surge of incredible release as fluid gushed between her legs.

Chapter 33

Bunny was whimpering and blubbering as Demetrius undid her restraints. He made quick work of them. Once she was released and he had gently removed the toys, he held Bunny close, kissing her forehead, her cheeks, and her nose. It was almost a ritual at this point, pulling her from the hole she was dropping into and bringing her back to reality.

Bunny felt like she was floating. Her body was lighter than it had ever been. She sighed softly and turned into his toned chest, pressing her cheek against his shoulder. Tipping her chin up, her lips brushed his earlobe as she whispered, "I need you."

He froze. This was a break in routine, and one he wasn't sure what to do with. Bunny knew he would be worried that he'd push her too far, and he was likely trying to tease apart whether this was a good idea or not. When the moment stretched on too long, Bunny took charge. She slid up and turned, dropping so that her legs were on either side of his and her core was brushing against his straining cock.

A small sound of protest could be heard as she leaned forward and captured his lips. Bunny pulled back, ducking her head to kiss along his collarbones and neck, waiting to see if he'd protest in earnest. Instead, Demetrius held her chin firmly in his hand and turned her head so he could look her in the eyes. "Is this what you want, Bunny? Do you want my cock?"

Her lower lip trembled as she responded, "Please, Demetrius. I need it. I… need your cock." The last part she tripped over, even now feeling a rush of discomfort at the vulgar language. Bunny heard him suck in a sharp breath, and then he was guiding her onto her back, placing her head gently onto a pillow. Bunny kept her eyes on his during the entire process, unable to look away. His gaze was so soft and she wanted to stay wrapped in it forever. She watched as he stripped off his pajama pants.

He must have gotten changed at some point. She couldn't remember.

Finally, he was sliding on top of her, Bunny shivering with joy at the slide of his skin against hers. She adjusted her legs, hitching them a little on his hips. Demetrius locked eyes with her again as he reached a hand down to position himself.

As he slipped his cock into her wet pussy, both of them let loose primal sounds. It was beyond incredible for Bunny. Instead of frying her nerves as she had feared, the earlier orgasms had only served to make her unbelievably sensitive.

She needed this. She needed to feel him on top of her, surrounding her, adoring her. Bunny was only pulled further into desire as she thought about his soft breath on her ear while one of his hands held hers gently. He began to move his hips, and she saw stars almost immediately.

"Fuck, you're so goddamn wet," He panted out between thrusts, kissing her neck lazily. Everything he was doing was so soft and tender, that Bunny's eyes began watering. She couldn't help but feel distinctly undeserving of the treatment. Demetrius picked up a quicker pace, letting go of her hand to brace himself against the mattress as his other hand pushed her knees back toward her chest. In this new position, he could ruthlessly slam into her while still maintaining eye contact.

Blushing heavily from equal parts bashfulness and desire, she met his gaze and wet her lips. He leaned down and captured them directly after. They stayed locked in that position, tangled entirely in each other, mouths moving in perfect synchrony.

Shock swept over her as she felt a familiar stirring in her stomach. Bunny didn't think there was any way she could possibly come again for him but had a feeling her body was about to make a liar of her. It made her moan into his mouth, and Demetrius took the opportunity to slip his tongue inside.

After a few passionate moments, Bunny broke the kiss to moan, "I'm going to come for you again." He began panting heavily, breath hitching, as he processed that information.

"God, I can't, I'm going to-"

"Come with me, baby."

And then they were both exploding, and

Bunny heard distantly the words she had been both dreading and pining for:

"God, fuck, Bunny, I love you."

It was squeaked out between his guttural groans. She moaned louder, the emotion in her chest encouraging a reaction between her legs. And then, almost without thought, she was responding.

"I love you, too- Fuck, God- I love you, Demetrius."

For a while, it was just his jerking hips and her twitching body and their panting and moaning. And then, gentle lips were searching hers out, and they were softly kissing once again.

Chapter 34

Her eyes had adjusted to the moonlight flooding the room, and everything was clear, although blanketed under that blue haze all things were early in the morning. There was no darkness to hide in.

Demetrius pulled out of her and they both grunted at the sensation. He then sat up, guiding her to do the same. She was practically in his lap, and he was holding her hands gently, staring into her eyes.

She felt like a cornered animal. Rooted to the spot, unable to run, but desperate to respond to the rapid patter of her heart by bolting.

"Bunny, I love you," He had taken a hand and held her cheek with it. She was still caught in the event horizon of his eyes, quickly sucked into what she was sure would be the most beautiful abyss in existence.

"It's okay if you aren't ready, baby," He said softly, stroking the apple of her cheek with his thumb. Always so patient, always so tender.

"No," She blurted out so strongly it shocked both of them, surprise lighting up their faces. Bunny blushed and cleared her throat awkwardly, eyes trained on the duvet.

She finally spoke, "I... I love you, too," It was eased out on a whisper of a breath. She felt him tense. Bunny shifted uncomfortably.

"Bunny..." His own whisper was brimming with emotion. She swore his voice cracked.

Tired of the space between them, Bunny threw herself forward, wrapping his arms around his neck, face buried in its crook.

"I love you, Demetrius Invanov. I do. I'm just such a bitch, y'know?"

Once he had gotten over the initial shock of her crushing hug, Demetrius wrapped his arms around her waist and chuckled.

"You're not a bitch, Bunny," He whispered in his ear, "That's why I have to make you *my* bitch every time you act out."

She gasped as though offended and then giggled, leaning hard into him. Demetrius kissed her pulse point. They stayed there, holding onto each other like there was nothing else in the world for a good while.

Fatigue was quick to settle in, however, and soon they found themselves crawling to the head of the bed, slipping under the covers, and falling asleep together.

The next morning, she didn't wake up alone. Instead, Bunny's sleepy eyes were met with a blurry Demetrius, holding her close and watching intently.

"Do you have any idea how creepy this is?" She said, squinting at him through one eye as the sun shifted in the clouds and brightness flooded the room. Bunny could feel her thighs sticking together uncomfortably and, with a growing flush, she remembered the previous night.

It wasn't being tied to a bed and forced to come until she almost blacked out that reddened her face. Instead, it was the confirmation of their feelings for each other. She fervently hoped he wouldn't remember, but knew he would.

"Do you want to get brunch out of the hotel today?" He asked through a yawn, covering his mouth as it stretched. Bunny moved to curl into his chest before nodding. Anywhere he wanted to go was somewhere she wanted to be. Besides that, brunch meant mimosas. She was greatly enjoying the day drinking that led to sloppy, intoxicated sex with the man she loved.

Loved.

Is that what this was? Bunny wasn't sure if she could apply that word here. It felt all too soon to commit herself to him, especially in the way he asked her to. The more she thought about it, the more she realized she had already given up to him every part of her that mattered.

What would handing over her heart hurt? Unless it was something that would be short-lived, in which case her heart would hurt a great deal. She wasn't ready to think about the possibility of living a life without him anymore.

They climbed out of bed onto the plush carpeting and did their morning stretches, a habit Bunny had introduced to Demetrius. It was excellent for the body and helped you wake up gently.

She put on a white dress with quarter sleeves, pairing an old black leather jacket of Demetrius' with a pair of leather ankle boots she had saved up for.

Demetrius had chosen a burgundy sweater, topped by a black jacket. His dark jeans ended at a pair of oxfords. When she caught sight of them in the mirror together, Bunny felt her throat tighten at the sight of him.

The restaurant was on the water, and their table had a gorgeous view of the sparkling waves. It was relatively calm today, but the cold was biting. She was happy to be in a heated room.

Brunch was served buffet style and both she and Demetrius drank a little too much and ate until they felt like they were dying. There was a haddock in lobster sauce dish they were desperate to get the recipe for in particular. The pair were falling over each other to get into the penthouse. They both jumped when the door opened, however, because a man was standing almost directly in front of it.

"What's up?"

The pair stood gaping until Demetrius finally broke the silence.

"Michael, what the fuck are you doing?"

"Oh, I was watching a movie."

"No, Michael. What the fuck are you doing in my suite?"

"Paula let me up. Real nice lady. Let her know I'm your assistant!"

"Goddamn it, Michael, you are not my assistant."

"Well, maybe I should do less assisting and then we'll see where you're at in life."

Bunny could feel her temperature rising as the two went back and forth. Finally, she snapped, "I really hate to get in the middle of your little lover's spat, but I'd love to get on with my day."

"Oh, shit, you brought your bitch?" He said around a mouthful of popcorn. He was holding a bowl full of it.

"Don't call me a bitch!" Bunny growled.

"Don't call her a bitch!" Demetrius sounded exasperated.

"Okay, Jesus, sorry! Well, what else am I supposed to call her?"

"My fucking name, you idiot!" Bunny shrieked through her hands, which were now covering her face. She was sure she was thoroughly flushed with the aggravation of being forced into the presence of the man in front of her.

"Well, you guys want to watch a movie?"

"NO," Both Demetrius and Bunny shouted.

Chapter 35

The three of them sat in the living room as a movie Bunny didn't care to watch play on the TV. She wasn't entirely sure how Michael had guided the situation to this point, but she was both impressed and vexed by the outcome.

She could tell Demetrius wanted to strangle his best friend. Over the months, Michael had been couch surfing and otherwise spending his time partying while he lost control of his life after dropping out of college.

He also came from money, but a different type of family altogether. She knew that things had been rough for him, as well, and tried to find sympathy for him as a result. Michael made that exceedingly difficult sometimes.

Bunny was lying with her head over the

armrest, her torso on the seat cushion, and her legs draped over Demetrius' lap. He had his arms crossed and was watching the movie with a tightened expression.

"So, Michael, what brings you here?" Bunny asked, looking at her manicure as she waited for one of his long-winded and often incredibly dumb answers.

"Well, my pops found my stash and he was not happy at all," He started, taking a deep breath for dramatic effect before continuing, "So, we had a little back-and-forth sort of situation, and he told me to get the fuck out, and I told him to shove a pole in his hole…"

He trailed off as though Bunny would have input into the ridiculous, frankly embarrassing story. Demetrius just sighed.

"Have you ever thought about being less of a fuck up?" Bunny asked absentmindedly, hiding a yawn behind the back of her hand immediately after. The mimosas were making her drowsy now that the buzz had worn off.

"Have you ever thought about being less of a bitch?" He shot back, but not unkindly. Bunny and Demetrius both groaned. Michael always meant well, even if he wasn't sure what he meant at all.

In Bunny's opinion, he always seemed just a little bit confused. He was a loyal man to the core, though, and even if he didn't understand what was happening, he would always have Demetrius' back.

They'd apparently been best friends since elementary school when Demetrius was the victim of bullying and Michael was the perpetrator. It was an unlikely companionship that bloomed during a sleep-away camp their parents sent them both to.

Ever since, he'd fought others alongside Demetrius, and also for Demetrius. He was his right-hand man. Bunny didn't care for Michael, but he was important to the person she cared most about. Because of that, she was willing to keep the peace.

They never got past snappy banter. In fact, it had almost become a comfortable relationship based on being snarky with each other. If Bunny wasn't an only child, she would have compared it to the way siblings bonded.

Bunny swung her legs over and sat up, looked up with a pout at Michael, and said, "Are you not going to even ask what we're doing?"

Michael had pulled his backpack over to him, which had been resting against the coffee table. From it, he pulled a few pill bottles and baggies. Without looking up from what he was doing, he replied, "Well, no. I think that's obvious. Fucking and drugs, probably."

Bunny groaned and Demetrius couldn't stop the laughter that escaped through his fingers, hand cupped over his face. That's when Bunny realized they had been having nearly sober sex, which also made things different from their usual routine.

She kind of liked it that way, if she had to compare the two. There was something so much more intimate about clearly remembering the play-by-play for the whole encounter. Michael looked up, looking between Bunny and Demetrius. Then, he asked, "You guys want any of this? I got a whole pharmacy in here. It's awesome."

Bunny was sure there was a vein popping in her head up until this point. She immediately seemed to have a change of heart by the look of her bright eyes and a small smile.

"Yeah, just go ahead and put me in a k-hole, dude," Demetrius sighed, folding his arms behind his head, fingers locked and supporting his head, which tilted back slightly.

"Ooh, yeah. I wonder what you would let me do…" Bunny reached over and put her hand on his thigh, tone playful.

Michael immediately said, "Ewww!" in the most juvenile voice possible. Bunny rolled her eyes. Demetrius smiled.

Eventually, they were all high on cocaine and molly. It was the mix of choice for several reasons, but mostly because it's what Bunny preferred. She knew there would be some intense sex whenever the two drugs were involved.

It was her favorite part.

Michael was talking a mile a minute, and she had been tuning him out for at least an hour. He and Demetrius were now in a hot debate about something. She didn't particularly care what had them bantering. Snuggled into his side, Bunny was completely content. Demetrius had his arm draped around her shoulders.

He wouldn't touch her in front of Michael, and Michael would never cross the line of asking to join them. Demetrius loved watching Bunny being used by his associates, but he had limits. Michael was like his brother, and he wasn't about to involve him in his deranged sexual exploits.

"Can we go to bed?" Bunny whined, looking up at him with pleading eyes.

"I think that can be arranged, honey Bunny," He murmured back, kissing her forehead.

"Eww!" Michael protested.

"Oh, shut up," Bunny groaned.

Demetrius stood, helping Bunny up alongside him. They said their goodnights, and Michael explained that he'd just camp out on the couch. Demetrius tried to convince him that it was really okay if he got his own room, and Michael responded that he really wouldn't be a bother.

By the time it was over, Bunny was buzzing with need and agitation. She practically dragged Demetrius along, heading directly for the bedroom. They may not have explicit interactions in front of Michael, but Bunny was intent now on making him regret his choice of sleeping arrangements.

Chapter 36

The next day, it was time to check out. Demetrius packed while Bunny supervised. He often assured her that supervision was strictly necessary since bag lugging required an expert eye. She was unimpressed with this explanation. However, there was a side of her that was becoming used to the treatment and was even beginning to soften to it.

Bunny loved the concept of being cared for in any capacity, even if she rejected it at every opportunity. Demetrius wasn't letting her run this time.

Michael had driven a BMW, apparently owned by his father. He still had access to his trust fund and toys, the man just didn't want to see him for a while. Michael and his father had an odd relationship, but Bunny didn't think anything of it until Demetrius pointed it out. She hadn't even thought of it as being necessarily unhealthy.

Needing a place to crash for a "little while," Michael proceeded to follow Demetrius the entire way back to his high rise. It had three bedrooms, one of them being a study, so Michael said with confidence that he'd fit in without disturbing anything.

Demetrius looked like he was trying to stave off a stroke as the exchange was happening. It wasn't that he didn't want Michael around. Instead, it was that he loved having the entire apartment to himself so he could fuck Bunny every which way possible on every surface available. Michael's presence would affect their ability to do that.

The day was pleasantly sunny, with soft rays shining through the sunroof. Bunny had her hair tied back with a green ribbon that matched her sweater. She was wearing the diamond choker Demetrius had gotten her.

Somehow, he had suckered her into keeping it. His mother had a hand in this decision, however. The bastard had mentioned casually that she didn't want the gift he had given because it was too luxurious.

She thought the woman would pass away on the spot. Immediately, Bunny was treated to an hour-long lecture explaining why she should not only accept but demand the way Demetrius treated her.

At the end of it, she profusely agreed, if only to get Katarina to settle down. He had threatened to do the same thing if Bunny ever refused a gift of his again. She figured he was mostly joking, but had occasionally used her safe word to signify that she was very serious about him backing off.

It was a little complicated to figure out how they fit together financially. Demetrius wanted to take care of her fully. Bunny wanted to pay her own way, just as she had been doing. Her worst fear was becoming too "kept" to stand on her own.

They had agreed to pick it up again at a later date and just feel it out for now. Bunny tried not to balk at him getting them fancy hotel suites or gifting her luxury lingerie, and he tried to lower his standards to avoid spooking her.

She was far more successful in this

compromise than he was, unsurprisingly. Bunny thought previously that she was a stubborn person. She had learned quickly that Demetrius was somehow infinitely more so than she was. Or, he was just far more patient, which was far more likely the answer.

Her music was playing at a moderate level, a sign that she wasn't interested in chatting with him. Demetrius always understood, never pushing her to interact when she was overwhelmed and needed a few moments to herself. She watched as the landscape changed, turning from country to city in what seemed like an impossibly short time. They pulled into the garage of the high rise, Michael close on their tail. Almost close enough for Demetrius to break-check him, but he didn't want to risk it in his new car.

Once they were in his apartment, Michael was shown to the study.

Demetrius had to take care of a few things out of the apartment, so he left Bunny and Michael behind to "bond," as he put it. Neither of them was thrilled with the arrangement, but Bunny did have a couple of things she wanted to do that would require somebody taller than her.

She intended to put Michael to work. He was anything but pleased about it. He demanded that they consume cocaine beforehand. She told him that it might be time to switch to crack if coke wasn't taking the edge off anymore and he was fiending for it already.

After the exchange, Demetrius kissed Bunny and told her he loved her so quietly she almost didn't hear him. Unable to respond, she hugged him tighter, and they stayed like that until Michael protested.

He left, leaving behind the unlikely pair that had a laundry list of chores to accomplish.

If there was one thing about Michael she admired, it was his dedication to whatever task he had been assigned. They were tidying the kitchen, putting things away, and wiping surfaces down. He was asking where things went, and otherwise making himself incredibly useful.

Chapter 37

Bunny first felt the stirrings of panic while she was dusting the top of the fridge on a ladder they kept handy so she could reach the top shelves. It was just a flutter in her chest, a missed beat, but it signaled so much more to come. She tried to brush it off, hoping if she just ignored things, she might be able to push through. Unfortunately, the feelings she had been fighting came back with a vengeance.

She felt like the walls were closing in. Every breath was a struggle, a reminder of the way her throat was painfully dry even while sweat trickled down her neck. Bunny climbed down from the ladder and held her chest, trying to breathe evenly. After a minute, Michael caught on.

"Yo, you good?" He was calm at first, but a worry set in when she gasped like a fish and grabbed the wall next to her.

"Ibuprofen bottle in purse," She managed to choke out, feeling tears prick at the backs of her eyes. *Not now, not now, please not now,* she begged internally as he rushed over to her bag, shuffling through it until he found what he was looking for.

Michael grabbed a water bottle off the kitchen table and ran back over to kneel next to Bunny, who had sunk to the floor. He gave her the water and the bottle, unscrewing the top of both. Bunny popped two of her Benzos into her mouth, washing it down with a quick sip. They sat there together in silence for a few minutes, Bunny sitting with her knees raised, head pressed into her thighs. Michael didn't seem uncomfortable so much as he seemed confused.

Finally, the silence was broken. "When I'm sad, I think about penny-farthings."

"I'm sorry?" Bunny lifted her head and blinked at him, struggling to understand where he was coming from.

"Yeah. Think about it. Name? Objectively hilarious. Aesthetic? Objectively hilarious. Bunny, it's fuckin' funny," He said through a hooting laugh. Bunny couldn't help herself. She joined him.

She never thought she'd be in a situation where Michael, of all people, was comforting her... and succeeding with his efforts.

"I'm going to be honest, Michael. I wasn't aware you even knew the word 'aesthetic', let alone how to use it in a sentence."

"Bunny, why are you always such a bitch?" He replied, but in a good-humored tone. He wasn't angry with her, instead simply pointing out a matter of fact.

She took another sip from the bottle, and almost spit out the water when he asked her. It wasn't untrue, especially with the revelations she had been having lately. Maybe she could stand to be nicer sometimes. Maybe even to Michael.

"Do you want to talk about it?" He offered, smiling as much as he probably figured he could get away with. This was the closest thing to an olive branch that had ever been extended between them.

Bunny sighed deeply, lifting her head. Everything had a slightly fuzzy quality to it now, including her emotions. It loosened her tongue.

Normally, she would have brushed him off.

"Demetrius punched my dad in the face when we went back to my parent's place for my birth certificate."

"He fucking what?" Michael said in disbelief, head whipping around to look at her.

"It's a long story. But the thing is that it was just… I don't know. I know he had it coming, but that's still my dad?"

"Yeah, I kind of get it," He replied softly, "I think I'd feel the same way if somebody popped off on my pops, even if he deserved it."

They sat in silence for a few moments, letting the small confessions linger between them. Am I bonding with him right now? Bunny thought to herself, bemused by the concept.

"Look, it's hard to see the person you've put so much trust in become violent. I think that's probably what's got you shaken up. But it's more than that. I'm not a fucking doctor, dude, but I think there's a lot of stuff going on up there"— He pointed at his head— "You got a doctor or what?"

"Yeah, I have a doctor. That's how I have the Benzos."

"Oh, shit, yeah. I just wasn't sure since

they're in the wrong bottle."

"I do that because it makes it less obvious that I'm taking a prescription medication. People get curious and I don't want to deal with it."

"Hell yeah, they get curious. Just send them to me," He was grinning now and Bunny found herself laughing. He was ever the salesman, always looking to offload the stock he kept on hand. Michael then cleared his throat and continued speaking.

"Bunny, he gets it. Demetrius gets it, I mean. He just has this thing where he gets what's going on in people's brains."

"You mean the ounce of emotional intelligence you're missing? Do you think he took it from you?"

"Can you knock it off for, like, five minutes?"

"Sorry."

"Just listen to me, alright? Demetrius has been through some shit. He's seen some shit, done this, done that. A lot more than you know. He'll understand if you talk to him. He's good like that."

Bunny soaked in his words. She knew they were true; she didn't need confirmation from an idiot burnout who she should be nicer to. But it did feel good to hear what she believed was true. This was especially the case because Michael knew him so well.

"I don't even know what there is to talk about."

"Violence is scary and don't do that?"

"I'm not sure anything would have stopped him."

"You'd be surprised. You've got him pretty pussy whipped."

She sighed, exasperated. Every time Bunny thought she liked him more, Michael would do or say something she deemed damning.

"I'm not saying it's a bad thing, Bunny, chill. He's happier since you came along. A lot more relaxed. Just seems more confident in himself, y'know?"

She mulled over the past few months, thinking about how his behavior had trended over time. As she recollected the events, she had to agree. There was a difference between when she'd met him and now.

"So, uh, why don't we finish up?" Michael asked, looking restless.

"Sure."

Chapter 38

A party had been planned, a formal introduction of Bunny to his business associates and friends, as he put it. She could feel a fluttering like wings waking up in her stomach as she approached her outfit. She was wrapped in a warm, fluffy towel that she was hesitant to part with.

The apartment was kept cool. As soon as she dropped the towel from her body, Bunny would be met with chills and goosebumps. She hesitated for a second before finally exposing herself to the air.

Bunny made a noise expressing her displeasure, and then quickly started putting on her strapless bra. From there, she slipped the dress over her head. Demetrius had specifically told her she wasn't to wear panties tonight.

It was held at his parent's house since it hadn't been rented out yet, but they were getting ready at his apartment. This was where everything was. Bunny had all but moved in, most of her belongings finding their way into his temporary home. He had been talking about buying a house lately. She wasn't sure how some of her things managed to turn up but had a suspicion he had been taking one item at a time and bringing them home with him.

She strode to the vanity he had purchased after seeing her eyeing it. After that fiasco, she had trained herself not to take notice of things she wanted when they were out and about. Bunny was grateful, but his making permanent changes to his space for her was something she was uncomfortable with.

Until now, of course. She'd relented and essentially lived with him full-time. The next semester, she was giving up her dorm room. They had talked about it and the drive to the college was worth it, especially since the barn was on the way.

Spending time in the bathroom was one of her favorite activities. It had unofficially become her space since she spent so much time lounging in the tub. She wished she was in it now, waiting for Demetrius to come home and join her. Instead, she was swiping a couple of cotton pads from a drawer and heading back out to get her makeup done. She'd go with something simple today, nothing too over the top.

The door to the bedroom opened, and she felt her heart seize as she jumped in shock.

"Easy, honey Bunny," Demetrius said, flashing a grin at her, "It's just me."

Her hand was clasped over her heart, but she felt a surge of warmth just by looking at him. She was sure now that what she felt was undoubtedly love. Bunny could practically hear the flood of oxytocin releasing in her brain.

He held a long, velvet box in his hands. She looked at it suspiciously, wondering what he had done now. Demetrius walked up to her, wrapping his hand around the back of her neck and pulling her in for a deep kiss that made her head spin.

"What's in the box, Demetrius?" She asked breathlessly once they parted. He wasn't going to distract her from the topic at hand.

"It's something to remember me by."

"Are you going somewhere?"

"No, but with this I can choke you from anywhere."

"You have my attention."

Demetrius opened the box, and inside of it glimmered a gorgeous choker. It was a single, thin rope of diamonds with an emerald hanging from the center like a tag. She opened her mouth to say something but shut it when nothing came to mind.

"I don't want to hear it. This isn't for you, Bunny, it's for me. You should be wearing my collar at all times, no matter the form it comes in. You'll wear this at the party and continue to do so until I switch it out for another."

She gulped, regarding him with apprehension. Bunny knew that he wouldn't be moveable at this moment, but she planned on bringing it up again later. She had plenty of reasons for not wanting to keep an expensive piece of jewelry she'd likely lose.

"Get in front of the mirror and face it," His voice was gravelly, a hint of desire showing through.

Bunny did as she was told. He came up behind her, put the box on the vanity, and picked up the necklace. Once it was positioned, he clasped it, then leaned forward so his neck was resting over the curve of her shoulder. They stared into the mirror.

"God, you're beautiful, baby. Look at you," He kissed her neck, "I hope you understand what this means. You're mine."

It was her turn to feel desire brewing between her legs, fanning a tingling sheet of heat through her core.

Unfortunately, it would have to wait.

Chapter 39

The garden was gorgeous. Demetrius had decorators come to ready it for the get-together he was throwing. Her collar was secure around her throat and it felt reassuring to Bunny. She fidgeted with it, a flush crawling up her neck at the memory of him clasping it behind her neck.

"You're mine...."

Demetrius was not the type to shower anything but luxury on the woman he had claimed. The interactions between his parents had proven that he had been raised this way.

Even still, she couldn't keep it. Bunny didn't want to know how much that choker was. She didn't care if it was symbolic. She wasn't going to wear somebody's salary around her neck. Besides, she didn't want to be responsible for keeping it safe.

Her hair was twisted up into a loose bun, strands framing the angles of her face.

Bunny felt gorgeous, sultry, sexy. As they sipped champagne and spoke to his friends, she hung on his arm, quiet except when she was spoken to directly. She was happy to let him do the talking for her. Bunny felt just fine being his arm candy.

Fairy lights were twinkling above, a net of them creating a false ceiling above. Ivy was threaded throughout, lending an ethereal aesthetic. Tulle had been incorporated in some of the decorations. Bunny was admiring her surroundings when Jeremy approached.

She blushed deeply upon meeting his eyes and diverted her own. All she could think about was his warm mouth bringing her over the edge while Demetrius held her in his arms. It was incredibly distracting. Jeremy didn't seem to be bothered, however, and he fell into easy conversation with Demetrius.

Around the time midnight hit, people started to depart. They said their goodbyes climbed into their luxury cars and drove away, leaving only a handful. Bunny was shifting uncomfortably now, her eyes scanning those left behind. Something felt off about the night, but she couldn't put her finger on it.

Demetrius appeared next to her, having come back from helping somebody back out of a tight spot.

"Hi, honey Bunny," He purred, nuzzling into her neck. She giggled and smiled, meeting his eyes.

"What's the plan?" She asked.

"Well, we're all going to gather in The Chill Room and play some drinking games until I decide to take you back to my room and fuck you until you can't walk." He said it so matter-of-factly that Bunny had a hard time responding, struggling for the words to describe how badly she wanted that but right now. In fact, she was beginning to get a little grumpy.

"Demetrius, why don't we head up a little early?" She asked, and he simply brushed her off with a little smile. She didn't like that little smile.

Chapter 40

He was standing behind her, admiring the way her body reflected the soft lighting. They had retired to his room, but not permanently. Instead, Demetrius told her to undress. She had done so excitedly, thinking he was initiating foreplay. Demetrius was doing no such thing.

She found herself stripped naked, her choker replaced by a thick leather collar. It took up most of her neck. She thought it looked gaudy. Demetrius told her that it would keep her neck safe from being touched. That was when she asked why she had to worry about that since they had worked through it, which was when she found out his plans for the rest of the evening.

Bunny was shivering. She was slick between her thighs even as her heart pounded an unforgiving rhythm. Her breathing was shaky. She was going to spend the rest of the night in the basement…

Like *this*.

He opened the door, holding out his arm. "Are you ready, Bunny?" He questioned, a devilish grin breaking out. She slowly made her way to him, knowing her face and chest were likely a deep shade of red.

They made their way down the sweeping stairs, arm in arm. He was mostly holding her up; at this point, Bunny felt like she was going to pass out. She felt herself separate from her body, felt the pull of her mind bring her up, up, and away. She breathed evenly as they approached the door to the basement, and then whimpered as they stopped in front of it.

"Bunny, it's okay if you don't want to do this," He whispered, pulling her into his arms. She pressed herself into his chest, feeling so much safer now that she was covered in some way. There was something about being so exposed that made even the simple gesture of a hug make you feel secure.

He kissed the top of her head, she whispered that she wanted it, and they made

their way downstairs. She first noticed the five men milling around. Suddenly, she heard his voice in her head, a vague memory of him telling her he was going to "pass her around."
Bunny gulped.

The men didn't take much notice of her, however. They all crowded to Demetrius, shaking his hand and clapping him on the shoulder. As a group, they strode over to the seating area around the fireplace. Which is when she spotted *it*.

"It" was a large wooden "X" standing in front of the fireplace, which was turned off. It had cuffs at each point, and she could guess what they were used for. She began to panic a little, realizing that this might be more than she had bargained for originally.

But Demetrius settled into his favorite chair, pulling her into his lap while he did. Bunny curled up there, facing him. She rested her head on the place where his chest met his shoulder. Smoke and cedar filled her nose. Bunny sighed happily.

The other men settled in, as well, passing around whiskey glasses and a glass tray. Bunny was already eyeing it as it came to Demetrius' turn. He took it and held it for her, whispering into her ear not to overdo it. Bunny scoffed at him and earned a stern look. Melting under his gaze, she cut a line about the length and width of her pinky finger and never left his eyes as she snorted the entire thing.

Demetrius narrowed his eyes but said nothing.

He took his line and passed the tray off to the person sitting to his right. Everybody had a glass of whiskey and they all began chatting about… whatever it was they were chatting about. Bunny was buzzing with excitement at the prospect of this new adventure, curled into Demetrius' arms, snuggling into his chest. That wouldn't last long, however. Demetrius soon raised his glass and said, "A toast, gentlemen?" They raised their whiskey in response.

"Here's to you, here's to me, may we never disagree. But if we do? Well, fuck you! Here's to me," With that, he lifted the glass and smiled as the men laughed heartily. They all drank. Bunny shifted as he began playing with one of her nipples, worrying it between his fingers. Her pussy's response was immediate.

"Well, now that we've gotten settled, I think it's time for the show," Demetrius started speaking again once they had all settled down, "Are we all ready?"

At the cheers of agreement, he patted Bunny's ass.

"Are you ready to make me happy, baby?" He whispered into her ear. Bunny whimpered but climbed off his lap. He led her over to the X and turned her around so she was facing the men. When she began to shake, Demetrius slipped a blindfold over her eyes.

"I think that'll help a little, honey Bunny. Let me see your hand."

He led her hand up behind her, to the top of one of the arms of the wooden structure.

"There's a button right here that will alert only me if it's pressed. If at any point you want this to end, press that button and I'll put a stop to it immediately."

Bunny gulped and nodded her head, He began securing her, cuffing her wrists first, and then her ankles. She was covered in a thin sheen of sweat and she could no longer control her breathing. Her pussy ached and she couldn't even press her thighs together to take the edge off of the burn.

He kissed her cheek and then began

speaking again. Bunny's other senses were heightened with the loss of her eyesight. Demetrius sounded louder now.

"Alright. You know the drill, my friends. We go around the circle and each person gets to choose a toy and how it's used. You get sixty seconds to make her come. If she does, you get free use of her for the rest of the night. If she doesn't, we move on to the next person."

Bunny's heart dropped into her stomach, and then a bit lower. The pulse between her legs was intensifying. She simultaneously wanted them to ravish her right that moment and wanted to run away screaming. This was insanity.

"I'm up first!" Demetrius said, clearly pleased, "And I think I'll go with this on the lowest setting. Get things kicked off! We don't want it to end too soon, do we?"

Her heart hammered as she tried to figure out what he was referring to. The blindfold was now acting as a barrier from whatever they were planning. If nothing was mentioned out loud, she had no way of knowing.

She felt fingers separating her labia, spreading her wide. Then, something hard and round pressed into her clit and the area surrounding it. She sucked in a breath and the buzzing began. It was a wand of some sort, and incredibly powerful even on the lowest setting. Bunny immediately started writhing, pulling on her restraints.

"Oh, my, I think she likes that. Don't you, gentlemen?" A low chuckle rose from the room, but it was quieter than before. She imagined it was due to the show she was undoubtedly putting on. Bunny was whimpering and mewling, throwing her head from side to side. It already felt like too much.

"Alright, time's up! Next?"

The vibrator was removed. She began panting in relief, taking in deep breaths as she readied herself. Footsteps sounded to her left and her heart rate picked up again.

"These look fun. What do you say, Demetrius? Leave them on the whole time? Just this once?"

After a moment, Demetrius said, "I'll allow it."

Bunny yelped and then groaned as a wet, warm mouth covered one of her nipples, and then another covered the other. Her entire body was on fire as the two men sucked, licked, and flicked the sensitive peaks until they were hard.

She moaned as cold air puckered them further when they removed their mouths. The sound was quickly replaced by a pitiful whimper as she realized they were tightening clamps onto her.

Oh, please, no, She thought to herself, the pressure already building furiously.

Chapter 41

Nipple play was one of her weaknesses and Demetrius knew it. She suspected the others did, as well. It would be his style to ensure they knew exactly how to torture her during this session.

She didn't know much about his associates or friends, just that a lot of them were also sexual deviants. Or, that's how it appeared. It was moments like these that reminded Bunny of the fact that she didn't know Demetrius as well as it felt like she did.

Somehow, that excited her all the more.

"Let's see. How about this? Not sure if we want to just leave that in, too, honestly."

Demetrius agreed it would be better and Bunny assumed her pussy would finally find some relief. However, when she felt fingers between her legs, they were from the back. Bunny yelped and lifted her hips, moving her ass away from the touch.

"Oh, sweetheart, let me help you," Demetrius crooned, putting his hands on her hips and shoving her back down so that she was pinned between him and the apparatus. Bunny whimpered and pushed her head forward, seeking contact with his face.

She was rewarded with his lips on her neck.

The fingers were back, coated in lube and searching for her tight rear entrance. Once they found it, they pushed slowly past the ring of muscle and began readying her. Bunny was keening now, trying to stay still but failing miserably as pleasure radiated through her.

"I think somebody is very close to embarrassing me in front of my associates," Demetrius whispered into her ear, his warm breath reassuring in this fragile moment. She could feel the man behind her stretching and readying her, and she tried to breathe through it. Something hard and large pressed at her entrance next, and Bunny groaned. As it slid inside her, she struggled to accept its size, whimpering and shifting under the strain.

"It'll fit, baby, shhh," Demetrius said, cupping her face with a hand and kissing her forehead.

Once it was inside of her she was gasping for breath, flexing and releasing. Demetrius hummed appreciatively. He kissed her forehead again and said, "Good girl."

The next couple of people chose the vibrator again, gently raising the speed until she was crying out in anguish, gasping for breath, begging them to stop. But she still didn't come.

"How will we even know? She's probably broken by now," A voice said.

"Oh, I'll know. Don't you worry," Demetrius responded.

And so the game kept on.

Finally, a familiar voice spoke up. "Alright, my turn. Hitachi. Full blast. Full minute, regardless of when she comes. Then, another minute after since she'll be mine at that point."

The entire group groaned and accused him of ending things too early. Bunny was soaked in sweat, hungry for Demetrius' rock-hard cock in her throbbing cunt, and wildly grateful to

Jeremy for getting to the end of things.

The wand was put in place again and Demetrius whispered, "Get ready, baby," into her ear as he turned it on full blast.

Bunny immediately screamed and started thrashing. She couldn't hear anything anymore outside of her own mangled cries. "Full blast" was more than she had ever thought was possible from a sex toy. It was consuming her. She was desperate to get away, and no matter how she moved her hips, the toy stayed lodged in place. Within seconds, a powerful orgasm was ripping through her.

Now she realized why he had only said two minutes. It would feel like a goddamn eternity. It was like sentencing somebody to a day in Hell– that single 24-hour period would feel like forever.

She realized tears were streaming down her face. She wasn't ready to use her safeword, though. When Demetrius leaned in to check, she told him to fuck off. He stayed quiet a moment before chuckling, "Oh, I'll be fucking something, Bunny."

Bunny was gasping and screaming and making noises she wasn't fully convinced were human. She gave silent thanks to him living on a large property; if neighbors could hear her, they'd absolutely call the cops. It sounded like somebody was being brutally murdered. She went completely slack as the wand was removed, shaking uncontrollably. The blindfold was removed and she looked up into Demetrius' face. Her eyes were drooping after she expended every last drop of energy she thought she had left.

Jeremy had walked up while Demetrius removed the nipple clamps.

"You can leave the plug alone, Demetrius. Knowing that tight, little ass is full does something for me… as I'm sure it does everybody else."

Another low chuckle. Demetrius didn't join them, however.

"Not too long. I don't want you wearing out my new toy before I get my fill of her."

Jeremy agreed and Bunny was released, collapsing into the man's arms. He held her tightly and kissed her forehead. "I think somebody's tired, Demetrius."

She buried her face in his chest and he bent, putting an arm behind her knees and scooping her up. Jeremy carried her to the couch, sitting down and draping her over his lap. Bunny squeezed her thighs together. There was still an unbearable, painful ghost lingering there, traces of the intense vibration.

The tray was back. Bunny greedily cut another line and sucked it down. She didn't want this to be over so soon. She needed to stay awake. She did notice, however, that Demetrius didn't take one for himself. He passed the tray on when it came to him.

Bunny felt the subtle rush of cocaine lift her out of her fatigue. It was a fake sort of energy, but it would keep her going until she was ready for things to be over. While she was certain this could be arranged again, Bunny wasn't sure she'd ever have the gall to go through with it.

She shuddered at the thought, a delicious shiver that felt like silk sliding across her bare body.

For a few minutes, they all sat there, chatting happily while Jeremy stroked her like she was a fucking dog. Bunny bristled a little at first but came to realize it actually felt incredible. He started at the crown of her head, dragging his hand down her back and to her ass.

She felt a hard slap and yelped, jumping

up. Her face was level with his, and Jeremy was grinning. Bunny knew the look on her face would spell murder. The look on his face told a different tale, however. Something was about to happen.

"I don't think it's fair that she's just for me, fellas," He said, holding her chin in his hand while he studied her closely, "Tell me, Bunny, how many cocks do you think you can fit in that pretty little mouth at once?"

Her eyes widened and her stomach dropped as her lips parted in surprise.

"It would be such a shame to keep all of this to myself. That pretty little face is just begging to be fucked. Who am I to refuse?" He said, swirling his whiskey, "On your knees, Bunny."

Chapter 42

The command came suddenly and fell on her like steel. She was crushed under the weight of desire and fantasy turned reality. Bunny climbed down from his lap and got onto her knees in front of him, sniffing as the post-nasal drip intensified. Jeremy put his whiskey down and began unbuttoning his pants.

She could hear sliding zippers and rustling pants. The rest of the men were exposing themselves. *He can't be fucking serious,* She thought in a panic, *Am I supposed to suck them all off?*

"You're so beautiful on those knees… but I think we're doing this all wrong," Jeremy said. He stood, taking Bunny by one of her hands and walking her back a few steps. She looked at him, puzzled.

"Obviously, she can't handle all of us at once. But one at a time seems so… poorly planned. Let's strategize!"

Jeremy helped her down, directing her to her hands and knees. Bunny could still feel the pressure from the plug filling her ass with every movement. He then got on his knees in front of her, the swollen head of his hard cock in front of her face.

"Chester, would you care to join me?" Bunny didn't bother looking to see which man was coming up behind her. She was too busy realizing what was about to happen. She was panting again, squeezing her eyes shut, and asking herself once again what the fuck she was doing.

When she could feel the other man position his cock against her pussy, she raised her eyes to Jeremy's face. He pressed the tip of his manhood against her lips, pushing forward until she opened her warm, wet mouth for him. Jeremy immediately groaned, throwing his head back.

Bunny nearly choked on his cock, however, because the man behind her also pressed forward, grabbing Bunny's hips to steady her and himself. He rocked slowly until he had worked himself into her up to the hilt. Bunny was frozen. Her mouth was crammed full, her ass was crammed full, her pussy was crammed full.

She was so *full*.

As the two men began thrusting, she began releasing throaty moans and writhing between them. They were now both jerking and wild in their motions Bunny was choking while she was moaning, trying desperately to handle Jeremy's entire manhood fucking her throat while she was being relentlessly pounded.

Hot cum shot out onto her tongue, coating her mouth in its thick, salty tang. The man pounding her pussy also came to his climax. She coughed and gasped as Jeremy pulled out of her mouth. Her jaw hurt.

The next two men took their position. Bunny shook with anticipation and worry. She wasn't sure she could keep doing this.

But she did. She took their hot loads, swallowing dutifully. The man who fucked her mouth checked, grabbing her face in a vice grip and telling her to open up wide so he could see if she swallowed like a good girl. She obeyed immediately. Afterward, she realized there were only two men left, and one was Demetrius.

Her savior stood in front of her, looking down fondly, admiring her. She was covered in sweat now, cum dripping down her thighs and out of her mouth.

Demetrius got on his knees and positioned his cock at her mouth.

She collapsed to the floor. Her entire body was sore and she felt entirely depleted of energy. Bunny wasn't even sure she could hold her head up. Demetrius was saying goodbye to his friends, thanking them for coming. If she was of a sound mind, she would have found it hilarious.

Hey, thanks for fucking my bitch, dude! "Come" again sometime! She thought to herself, giggling softly. Maybe there was still a little energy left after all. She heard Demetrius' approach before she heard his voice. But, before either, she smelled his scent in the air. It was almost as though she was attuned to it now. Worse than that, she actively craved it.

"Look at how filthy you are, baby," He crooned, tucking some of her hair behind her ear, "You're fucking filled with cum."

He leaned down to whisper in her ear.

"And I know you loved every minute of it. I saw your face. I know how badly you wanted to be used like the little fuck toy you've become." Bunny hummed in agreement. She was too tired to do anything else. So, Demetrius gathered her in his arms, kissing her temple.

"You're amazing, Bunny. Always such a good girl for me. You made me so happy tonight."

She felt like she was glowing under his praise, even as every hole throbbed from the use and abuse she had taken. None of it mattered. Somehow, as long as she was his good girl, she didn't care.

Chapter 43

It was early in the morning. Snow was falling softly outside, dusting the world with fat, fluffy flakes. Inside, Bunny lounged on the floor in front of the fire. Demetrius was making popcorn and hot chocolate in the kitchen. Floor-to-ceiling windows covered the wall, providing the perfect view of the city in the middle of what was said to be the blizzard of the century.

She had heard that before.

Regardless of their doubts, she and Demetrius had stocked up on snacks and entertainment, ready to buckle down should the snow pile up. They were prepared for a cozy cuddle in front of the fire followed by board games and movies.

She fiddled with the collar around her

neck. She had taken to always wearing it when they were home. It made her feel secure and it pleased Demetrius. The smooth, black leather was lined with fur, with a little heart tag at the front. He had it handcrafted and insisted the inner lining be plush so the leather wouldn't rub her skin raw. Bunny was also naked, another habit she had picked up living with him. The exposure left her uncomfortable in any other situation. But with Demetrius, she felt secure.

In some parts of her mind, she thought she could get used to this life. She knew that if she wanted to quit school after her Bachelor's and be one of those girlfriends who stays at home and does pilates, he'd support her wholeheartedly.

It sounded lovely; lazing around all day, going to the barn whenever she wanted to, being a pampered pet to a man who adored her. Bunny just couldn't do it. That wasn't part of her plan, and she wasn't making changes just because a man could take care of her… But it was nice knowing she could give up at any time and live a charmed life.

Part of the pressure she was always under was the knowledge that she couldn't fuck up. She didn't have family waiting to bail her out, and she sure as hell didn't have a backup plan. Bunny had money saved, but not enough to get her through something catastrophic. When she finally realized that Demetrius was here to stay and that she now had a soft landing if she faltered, Bunny relaxed immensely. Everybody had noticed.

He had brought up the idea of marriage a few times, but Bunny had brushed him off. It was far too early to think about that. Although, and she felt shameful for thinking it, marrying him would set her up for life. After all she'd been through, didn't she deserve something good? However, she wasn't of the mind to marry a man based on what he could provide her. No, Bunny needed something more than that to win her hand. She didn't know what, but she'd know it when she saw it, and that's all that mattered to her.

Demetrius came around the corner carrying a tray with a bowl and mugs balanced precariously. She smiled sweetly at him, drinking in the sight. He set the tray down on the coffee table, glancing over at her with those soft eyes. She loved how his face relaxed whenever she was in view. They were dark as onyx, but there was a light that sparked for her and her alone.

His cologne hung in the air alongside the warming scent of crackling firewood. She stretched out luxuriously, spreading her body over the plush rug he had placed on the hardwood floor just for her. She loved toasting herself in front of the flames.

"Come here," Demetrius called out, kneeling at the edge of the rug and holding his arms out. Bunny obliged without a second thought, throwing herself into his open embrace. He wrapped his arms tightly around her, pressing his face into hers.

She was desperate for the sanctuary he offered. Bunny felt like she was harbored from any storm that could come her way, no matter how it howled or raged. If Demetrius was holding her, there was nothing that could touch her. When she was with him, she could be as small and fragile as she felt. His hands were strong only in their protection of her, turning tender in a heartbeat when she reached for him.

With a small kiss on her forehead, Demetrius breathed out, "I have a surprise for you later."

Bunny immediately perked up, but he said nothing more on the matter and she wasn't about to push. He loved keeping her guessing, even when she wasn't normally a fan of surprises. She simply melted further into his arms and sighed contentedly.

He let go of her after a few more moments. Their attention turned to the tray Demetrius had brought over and they took their respective mugs. It was a rich, creamy blend of gourmet chocolate and steamed milk. He had expensive taste, and Bunny was just fine with reaping the benefits.

The warmth from the drink made her hands tingle pleasantly as she sipped at it, pulling back with a whipped cream dot on her nose. Demetrius took a napkin and wiped it off, Bunny closing her eyes and soaking in the attention. Their relationship was more than something deranged and sexual. It extended far beyond the bedroom. He took thorough care of her in every situation, and she deferred to him with an ease she had never known. For as long as she could remember, Bunny had been a control freak.

Demetrius had changed all of that.

She was able to let go and allow him to make the decisions. Stress had lifted from her shoulders in rolling waves as soon as she discovered the power she held even in submission. The truth was that she ran the show; everything was done to her comfort level and specifications. Demetrius watched her closely in all interactions to ensure her safety and consent.

He had a talent for figuring out where her limit was and pushing her until she was just there. She loved him for his ability to gauge when she would use her safe word and end things right at the ledge. It had become something easy for him after a few instances where she'd ended a session early.

With his back to the coffee table, Demetrius nudged her with a hand to curl up under his arm. She slid over, taking care not to spill her hot chocolate, and made a small noise when he began tweaking and circling one of her nipples. His silk shirt felt incredible against her naked breasts and belly, sliding smoothly against the exposed skin.

She'd squirm the entire movie as he worked her into a frenzy. By the end of it, she'd be laying between his legs, whimpering as he played with her pussy, keeping her just at the edge without being allowed to tumble over.
He had referred to it as "free use." Bunny had

readily agreed that she liked the sound of it; both the practice and what it entailed.

They had been following the lifestyle since she had moved in with him, leaving her dorm behind with a heavy heart and frayed nerves. Demetrius had repeatedly told her that it was going to be okay and that she'd be on the lease so she could be on equal footing with him. Bunny wouldn't have agreed to the living arrangement if she hadn't been named a legal resident. It was too much risk otherwise.

The movie dragged on and Demetrius continued to tease and pleasure her, whispering dirty things into her ear now and again. She couldn't have told you what the movie was about— it simply wasn't what her attention was trained on. Once the credits rolled, Demetrius whispered in her ear, "I think it's time for your surprise, my love. The snow doesn't seem to be getting worse. Get ready to go out. Wear that little black dress I love."

Chapter 44

Bunny slipped into the aforementioned dress, which clung to every curve and stopped mid-thigh. The shoulders were slouched, and it was a sleeveless number that made her look irresistible. Her long hair was perfectly curled and brushed through until it fell in soft, wavy coils.

She'd even done her makeup: a cute cat eye wing, red lip, and soft blush brushed over her cheeks and nose. Bunny used a light foundation to avoid covering up the dusting of freckles across her face. Demetrius loved to tell her that he planned to someday kiss every single one of them.

When he came to collect her from the bedroom, he slipped a day collar around her neck. It was the simple band of diamonds with the emerald which clung tightly against her throat. Bunny was fine with collars at home or in like-minded company.

However, she was uncomfortable with random strangers or people she knew knowing about her new lifestyle. Demetrius made sure she had a wide range of options to wear that still marked her as his even while out in public. Even if laypeople wouldn't recognize a day collar or their dynamic, it was enough for Demetrius that he and Bunny knew.

From there, he took her arm and they headed out the door.

The club was plain from the outside, betraying none of the debauchery happening behind the closed doors. Demetrius had explained that it was a business you knew nothing about unless you were in a certain circle. Naturally, he was an important member of it.

Bunny realized suddenly that they were headed into an establishment made for play. She paused uncomfortably at the door, Demetrius squeezing his hand around hers. He turned, his face offering reassurance. She obliged him and followed behind.

The inside screamed elegance. It was a space fully outfitted in black; satin, leather, and wood. Bunny found herself admiring the mood that it set; immediately, her mind was shifting gears, and low heat in her belly signaled the change. Demetrius still had her hand as he led her forward, walking down a long hallway. They made their way into a door at the end, which opened into a smokey den filled with men in suits milling around. She recognized most of them.

In that instant, Bunny felt the heat build into a bonfire. She was obviously expected to perform for him and his friends tonight, and she lusted after the idea. The concept of being so vulnerable in front of so many, all eyes trained on her as she was commanded to pleasure herself and those around her, was one that always made her heart race.

A little pressure on her hand made Bunny realize she had been frozen for a few seconds. At his signal, she began timidly making her way forward, eyes downcast to avoid catching the gaze of any one man. Demetrius brought her to sit on his lap as he rested on a Victorian-inspired sofa.

The room was decorated similarly to the entryway. Satin curtains hung sheer, waving gently as people passed close. The sofa they were sitting on was accompanied by a few chairs, all situated around a coffee table. Everything was black, the wooden flooring gleaming from wall to wall except under the chairs and couches where a plush, burgundy rug added a splash of color to the gothic surroundings.

"I think you're a little overdressed, don't you?" A sultry murmur that made loose strands of hair sway next to her ear. Bunny gulped, scanning the space around her and noticing that quite a few men were staring her down with eager eyes.

They were all dressed to impress, each with a drink in hand. Demetrius demanded excellence from those around him. This was especially true when the love of his life was on the table.

He lifted her by the hips so that she was standing on wobbling legs between his spread legs. Demetrius then took the sleeves of her dress and slipped them from her shoulders. The dress fell with a hushed sound to pool around her heels. He then unclipped and threw her strapless bra to the side. Bunny was left entirely nude and shivering, hunching in on herself as the burn of being perceived in such a state settled over her body.

Within moments, Demetrius had reached forward, wrapped an arm around her waist, and pulled Bunny back so that she landed square in his lap. She could feel his cock, rock hard, pressing into the line of her ass. Bunny simply squeaked as he threaded his hand into her hair and pulled back with just enough force to make her scalp sting. She whimpered gently as he kissed her cheek before saying, "Don't hide, Bunny. I want that beautiful body on display. That's what we're all here for tonight."

Her cheeks were burning, but Bunny pulled her arms down, gripping either one of his thighs as she bared her breasts and stomach to the crowd.

They were back to talking amongst themselves. There was a low mumble as the colleagues mingled, some of them coming to sit in the chairs to engage Demetrius in light conversation. He slid his hands between her knees and pulled them gently so that she was completely spread to her audience.

She settled into the position, thinking to herself, *Let the games begin.*

Chapter 45

Bunny's collar was comfortably snug against her neck. Aside from that, she was still completely naked, except for the plug she wore in her ass. Demetrius had told her she'd never looked more beautiful in her life. She was sitting on her legs next to his chair, hands on his lap and head tilted slightly as she looked up at him.

Demetrius looked down, smoothing her hair with a hand and then lifting her head by gently gripping her chin. His sultry eyes devoured her body as he scanned her, taking in the sight of something only he had the right to touch unless special permission was granted.

Bunny heard the door to the room open, surprised that more people were trickling in. When the newcomers appeared, her jaw almost dropped: there was another woman, in the nude with a collar, walking in behind a tall man. He was grinning from ear to ear as he saw Demetrius.

"Niles! It's so good to see you, man, how are you?" Demetrius' welcome was genuinely warm.

"Do you think they'll be good company for each other?" Niles asked, motioning at Bunny and then to the woman behind him. Demetrius nodded and agreed that he did think as much.

The other woman ended up being directed to sit right next to Bunny, so close their hips were touching. She felt her core tightening, her heart picking up speed. She couldn't believe he had done this. The woman next to her was perfect.

"Bunny, my love," She looked at him as he spoke, "This is Nile's pet. Her name is Kitty. Isn't that fun?" Bunny stole a glance at the other woman, feeling herself blush deeply as she realized that Kitty was playing with her nipples… While staring directly at Bunny.

Demetrius leaned down, whispering into her ear, "Why don't you be a good girl and go play with the nice Kitty?"

She gulped. The prospect was terrifying but she desperately wanted to touch the other woman. She was gorgeous. Alcohol was flowing freely and they had already dipped into the party favors. Demetrius had been strict on her consumption and she now understood why. He wanted her to fully consent to this. It was something she wanted, but she hadn't explicitly told him as much. He had simply taken it upon himself to go out and find a woman who fit the bill after their conversation.

She goddamn *loved him* for it.

Bunny turned so she was facing Kitty, only to find a pair of perfect tits pushed almost into her face. Kitty was on her knees, leaning over Bunny, looking at her with a soft smile. Briefly, she hoped that Kitty had been informed that she would have to take the lead.

The next few moments proved she had.

Chapter 46

Kitty placed a hand along Bunny's cheek, pulling her forward. Bunny obliged without a second thought, letting the woman lead their lips together. Kitty had a soft mouth, and she tasted faintly of something fruity. The kiss was chaste at first, but soon it blossomed into a feral dance between two deeply horny women.

She felt Kitty's fingers at her core and gasped, hips rocking into the woman's hand. Kitty slipped two of them inside of Bunny, crooking them as she gently flexed her hand, kissing Bunny's neck. She felt herself coming undone. Before she knew it, Bunny was bucking her hips, gasping for air, and begging for more.

Demetrius leaned down and snatched her up. Bunny was pissed.

She began fighting him, thrashing around and growling, before he flipped her over his lap and spanked her a few times. A few laughs rose from the gentlemen around them, all dressed as though they were there to broker deals. Instead, they were drinking beer and watching two sex slaves fuck.

Startled, she realized that's the category she fell under in this situation. Is that what I am? She thought, bewildered.

You're naked in a basement filled with leering business associates of your lover with a collar around your neck. What the fuck do you think you are? Bunny realized, heart beginning to pick up.

Demetrius was being passed a tray. He put it on her back since she was still draped over his lap and began to blow a line from a rolled-up hundred-dollar bill. She wasn't sure what was on offer, but it was likely cocaine. That was the drug of choice in these circles.

Bunny would kill for a little ecstasy.

The tray was taken and Bunny turned her head to look at him, catching his eye with hers. He leaned his head down to whisper in her ear, "What do you think you've done to deserve it, baby?"

"Please, Demetrius?" She whimpered, face pleading for the rush that tray would provide.

"Alright. But you're going to sit in my lap and spread those legs," Bunny began panting at this point, "and Kitty is going to eat you out while you take your line… and for a little while after."

She was now on fire, her entire body burning with a low, deep heat that vibrated and buzzed. He helped her sit up, and then she was facing forward in his lap. He reached his hands down, took either leg under the knee, and spread her legs wide so that her calves were resting on the arms of the chair. Bunny leaned back so that she was pressed into his chest, something to comfort her while she was overwhelmed.

The tray came back, and she felt warm hands on her thighs. When Bunny looked down, Kitty was there, watching her with kind, soft eyes. She had obviously been treated to something already since she was sniffling gently.

A line was cut and prepared for her, but Demetrius stopped them.

"She can cut her own line. Mix it back up."

Bunny sucked in a breath. That had not been part of the deal. Demetrius was doing this on purpose just to add to his entertainment.

"Alright, my love. It's time for the show. Remember the rules," He whispered into her ear as the tray was lowered and held for her. Bunny picked up the heavy credit card, staring at the mess of powder on the glass.

Kitty ran her tongue through Bunny's slit.

She gasped, jerking.

A laugh rose, Demetrius joining in with a deep chuckle.

"Bunny, love, if you do that while you're snorting, you'll get it everywhere," He grabbed her hair and pulled her head back, before saying, "And then I think we'd have to take some drastic measures. Wouldn't we, gentlemen?"

The small crowd let out a low cheer, agreeing wholeheartedly. Bunny gulped. The threat had been made, and she knew every person in that room except for her was praying she'd, well, blow the blow. Judging from the gleam in Kitty's eyes, she was of the same mindset.

Bunny took a shaky breath and began cutting the line again, panting heavily as Kitty began to run her tongue up to Bunny's clit, and then back down to her entrance again. She did this several times, and Bunny was reeling. Her shaking hands successfully separated a line and she took the rolled-up bill from Demetrius.

Shivering as Kitty continued her tireless assault, Bunny tried to get through the line as quickly as she could. First, she tested either nostril, holding either side while she inhaled through the open one, to see which would be better to blow with. Her right was the winner. Bunny leaned down to take the line and then her head shot back again, mouth opening and a choked moan pouring out. Kitty's tongue was circling her clit, bringing her a heady pleasure that demanded attention. With great effort, she managed to push her head back down, breathing in hard through her nose.

Bunny snorted like lightning, flashing through the process more quickly than she ever had, before throwing her head back and crying out as Kitty slipped her curling fingers into her heat. She let her head roll back, hips pressing upward into Kitty's mouth. Bunny moaned through a wide-open mouth, gasping when Demetrius moved his hands up to play with her nipples. He loved lazily pinching and pulling and rubbing the sensitive nubs while he watched the shows he organized.

Bunny began writhing, and her hands shot down to thread through Kitty's thick red locks. She pulled softly, mewling with delight as the woman expertly ate. When she added suction, Bunny was sure she'd spill over the edge into ecstasy.

"D-demetrius," She whimpered out, "C-can I co-come?"

"Yes," His voice was low and dripping with desire. Bunny exploded into an orgasm, her entire body arching until Demetrius had to hold her back from slipping off the chair entirely. Kitty leaned back, apparently satisfied with her handiwork, wiping her mouth with the back of her hand. Bunny decided at that moment that Kitty was the most beautiful creature she had ever seen.

And she wasn't done with her.

She scooted forward, swatting away Demetrius' hands when he tried to restrain her. Bunny never took her eyes off the deep blue gaze of the woman sitting in front of her. The men oooh'd at her display of defiance. In response,

Demetrius threw up his hands and said, "Well, gentlemen, I guess the show isn't over."

It was Bunny's turn to hold Kitty's face. She pulled her forward and pressed their lips together. Within seconds, Bunny's body was crushed into Kitty's, breasts rubbing and hands searching between them. Each was focused entirely on the pleasure of the other— it was an equivalent exchange at its finest.

Bunny's blood was on fire. She still wasn't sure she wanted to put her head between Kitty's legs, but kissing her was so nice. She was soft and supple and there was so much more to hold onto than with men.

Demetrius leaned forward to separate them, and Bunny turned, pulling Kitty with her. She whispered, "Follow my lead," into the woman's ear before looking up at Demetrius. He was visibly puzzled, especially as both women raised to their knees, pushing him back into the chair. Bunny began unbuttoning his pants, a task made harder because his thick cock was fighting for freedom, making the space tight.

As soon as he sprang free, Bunny leaned forward to capture him in her mouth. She bobbed her head a couple of times before pulling off so Kitty could give him the same treatment. Then, they both began to lick together, tongues dragging against his dick and each other as they both moaned and panted. The room was dead silent outside of the noises the two women made while they pleasured Demetrius.

Bunny could tell he was ready to go over the edge, so when he put his hands down and grabbed both women by the neck, she didn't fight him.

"Niles, come get your bitch," He croaked out, putting his dick, now a shade of purple, back into his pants.

"Fuck you, buddy," Kitty laughed good-naturedly, standing up with Niles' help. Demetrius waved his hand, dismissing the room, and people began to file out. Bunny watched only him, however, as he sat on the chair.

Chapter 47

He leaned down, putting his hand gently around her throat, and she tensed. He waited. She relaxed. He pulled her toward him. Once her face was in his, he brushed his nose against hers before beginning to speak.

"Everybody is gone for now, honey Bunny. I can't wait to taste that sweet pussy," He paused here, smiling wickedly, "But I wonder… Who eats you better? Kitty? Or me?" Bunny flushed deeply as she began to squirm, remembering how incredible the woman had been while she used her mouth to pleasure her. It was almost as good as what Demetrius did.

"You," She whimpered, pushing forward to kiss him. Instead, Demetrius pulled away. Bunny looked as wounded as she felt. He let go of her neck and stood, pointing at the couch.

"Lay over the back of it, with your ass right at the top, Bunny."

The warmth building in her pussy surged in a flood of desire that had her thinking of all the delicious ways he could twist and turn her body, fucking her from every angle possible. Her smile turned mischievous as she realized how well-behaved she had been… and how quickly that tide could turn. Bunny saw the look in his eyes when she caught his gaze out of the corner of her eye. His eyes were dark, and his smile a knowing one that told her he knew exactly where this was going.

Within moments, she was racing across the room, a grin splitting lips still plump with desire. Demetrius gave chase immediately. They ended up on either side of the couch, sizing each other up, frozen as they both waited to see what the other would do.

Demetrius broke the stand-off by rushing forward, stepping onto the couch, and vaulting himself over the back. Bunny shrieked in delight, turning on heel and trying her best to get away. An arm encircled her waist and she gasped as Demetrius brought her to the floor. They landed hard, but Bunny giggled even as pain shot through her back.

"You're going to regret that, Bunny," He murmured into her ear, "Oh, do I have plans for you."

Her giggles melted into a low moan as his hand wrapped around her throat, squeezing gently. Waves of warmth traveled the length of her body, her core responding with gentle flutters. Bunny loved the chase, but she loved what he did to her afterward even more.

Her hands and feet struggled gently against the restraints she had been placed in, cuffs on each attached securely to the bed posts. Bunny made a soft, pathetic noise, eyes fixed on Demetrius as he laid out the toys he planned to use on her.

The sheets were jersey knit and felt deliciously soft under her skin. He had placed a fluffy pillow underneath her head and checked in with her before continuing the scene. She'd given her explicit consent and assured him she didn't want it to end.

Demetrius paid her no mind as she writhed and whimpered. Instead, he turned his head briefly to firmly say, "Hush." With that, he was back to readying the growing pile of items that would bring both pleasure and pain.

The door opened and she looked over, puzzled at the intrusion. Her heart promptly began beating faster. Four men were walking through, all wearing wicked grins as they eyed her struggling body. With a sinking feeling, she realized where this was going.

Soft chatter filled the space as they poured drinks and talked amongst themselves. Demetrius had finished his task and joined them, accepting a scotch neat with a smile from one of the newcomers.

"Shall we?" He said, lifting his glass to hoots and cheers that echoed in the spacious room. Bunny's heart hammered a heavy beat in response. Her center pounded just as hard.

The small group made their way over, fanning out around the bed so she was surrounded. Their hungry gazes raked over her body and she wished she could curl in on herself. Demetrius had made a point to work with her on becoming comfortable with nudity. However, it was still difficult to cope with the humiliation of being exposed in front of so many strangers.

Looking up, she realized Demetrius was holding a blindfold. Her eyes locked onto his and he smiled reassuringly. Bunny closed her eyes and gulped quietly as he leaned down to place the fabric over her eyes. As he leaned down, he whispered into her ear, "Remember, my love, that you have a safeword you can use at any point. I'll be watching and listening."

And then, the world went dark.

With the loss of her vision, Bunny knew she would feel everything so much more intensely. Sweat began to gather on her forehead and she felt a hand softly smooth it away, brushing hair back from her face. She wasn't sure who had done it, and the thought made her heart flutter.

The buzz of a vibrator shifted her attention away from the discomfort of not knowing. She panted in anticipation, body tensing and the restraints becoming taut as a result. She didn't have to wait long, however, because, in the next breath, powerful vibrations were ripping through her pussy as the toy was pressed against her clit.

Bunny's hips bucked as she gasped, a

strangled moan exploding from her open mouth. Her hands balled and opened as she struggled to hold onto herself. A warm mouth began lapping at her breast, teasing the tender peak until it pebbled beneath the fervent ministrations. Something pressed against her entrance and she whimpered in response. Somebody stroked her cheek, whispering gentle praise into her ear. It did little to bring her comfort. It wasn't Demetrius.

The dildo pressed in and filled her slowly. She felt the beginnings of an orgasm building in her belly, the walls of her pussy fluttering frantically.

And then, a hand around her throat.

Bunny sucked in a breath and then screeched her safeword, and the room exploded into a frenzy she was unable to see. However, she could hear Demetrius bellowing.

"You rapist piece of shit," The words filled the room, overpowering every other voice, "I'll fucking kill you!" His voice was frantic to her ears, a vein of rage in them that she had never heard before. There were a few soft thuds, and then more yelling. The other men were now panicking, calling out to Demetrius, telling him to back off before he ended up in prison. Then running, what she suspected was the door opening, and more running.

"Baby, I'm so sorry," Demetrius sounded distraught, as though his world was crashing down around him. She knew he would take this to heart. It was his job to protect her in these scenarios. This time, he had failed to do so.

"Help me get these off!" The command was barked out and she felt hands at her wrists and feet, undoing the restraints. As soon as they were off, her body snapped into a ball, and she began sobbing.

Chapter 48

Her crying had subsided into sniffles and the occasional hiccup. Demetrius was sitting on the bed with his back to the headboard, holding her close as she recovered. He stroked her hair and peppered kisses across her face, whispering gently to her about how much he loved her and how sorry he was.

"Why- why did you c- call him a rapist?" She managed to choke out in stutters, still reeling as her skin crawled. She could still feel that man's hand around her throat, and every time she realized this, panic set in anew.

"Because he is, Bunny," Demetrius murmured, "He saw your papers. I talked to all of them beforehand. He knew what he was doing, and what he was doing was ignoring your limits. You expressly did not consent to having your neck touched. In fact, it was the opposite. If somebody does something sexual to you knowing that it's off the table, they're assaulting you."

She shivered, suddenly feeling cold and drained. Demetrius tightened his hold, burying his face in her hair and breathing in her scent. Her heart rate had begun to slow and the adrenaline was wearing off. Now, she was just tired.

"I need you to tell me what you need, baby," His voice was soft and soothing, "How do you need me to take care of you?"

At that moment, her heart felt full to bursting. Despite the terror that had seized her, and the way remnants of it were still lingering in her chest, Bunny began to feel the comfort of safety settling over her.

This man loved her. He would do anything for her. That knowledge gave her the strength to push away from him slightly, look him in his beautiful, dark eyes, and simply say, "I want to go home."

The trip back was a blur. As soon as the words left her lips, Demetrius had sprung into action, helping her get dressed and then carrying her bridal style to the car. He slid her into the passenger seat and buckled her in, brushing a strand of hair from her face and lingering for a soft kiss before closing the door.

Bunny leaned against the doorframe, her head heavy and empty all at the same time. Her favorite songs played softly over the speakers, but she couldn't place a single one. Instead, her fuzzy brain focused on numbing the feelings that threatened to overwhelm her.

Once home, Demetrius opened the door for her and helped her out. Her feet were bare—she hadn't wanted to put her heels back on. Like a small child, she had kicked away his hands and whimpered, "No," when he tried to slip them on her feet. He scooped her back up and made his way up to their penthouse. Bunny buried her face in his neck, drinking in the cologne he lightly spritzed on his skin every morning. There was still a trace of it left, mingling with a scent that was entirely his own. She sighed, relaxing further.

Michael wasn't there and hadn't been in some time. Neither of them was sure where he had gone, but she was happy that they would have the place to themselves. Bunny wasn't sure she could handle having him around while she was like this.

Once they were inside, Bunny began slipping her dress off again. It fell to the floor with a "whoosh" in the otherwise silent room and she felt herself settle down. Demetrius came up behind her.

"Can I touch your neck, baby?" He asked gently, and Bunny stiffened before nodding. There was still a vein of panic wrapped tight around her heart, which picked up speed when she felt his hands brush against her nape. Demetrius undid the diamond collar she had worn, slipping it off gently and tossing it onto the entryway table.

She turned and pressed herself into his chest, her arms around his waist. Demetrius returned the embrace and kissed the top of her head.

"I want my collar," She whimpered, voice muffled in his shirt.

"That's my girl," He crooned in response.

He snatched her house collar off the same table. They left it there so she could put it back on as soon as she stepped through the door. As he slipped it around her neck and buckled it, Bunny felt herself relax. It was a consistent reminder of their bond and his commitment to taking care of her. Some might have looked at it derisively as a mark of ownership, but Bunny saw it for what it was: the ultimate symbol of his affection and dedication to their dynamic.

They made their way over to the sectional to lounge together. It was large and looked more like a bed than a couch. Both she and Demetrius were able to stretch out across it. Today, they curled up tightly with each other.

"Are you hungry?" He asked, hugging her tightly. Bunny nodded into his chest and he pulled out his phone, scrolling through their options.

"Thai?"

"No."

"Indian?"

"No."

"Italian?"

"That's the one."

He smiled and began punching in the order. Bunny closed her eyes and listened to the soft sound of his heartbeat, training her attention on her senses. Although the space and time were making things easier, she felt numb from the earlier encounter.

The assault, She thought to herself, mulling over the word. It was odd. Bunny wouldn't have considered it that. She would have written it off as an honest mistake made in the heat of the moment and now wasn't sure how she felt about any of it.

"What's going on, Bunny?" The deep timbre of his voice broke her out of the trance her thoughts had lured her into.

"Nothing."

"It's not nothing, Bunny. Talk to me."

She sighed and shifted, pushing away so that she was sitting up, refusing to look at him.

"I don't want to talk about it. I want to talk about literally anything else."

"Alright, that's okay, baby. What do you want to talk about?" His voice was soft and soothing, accompanied by a hand that reached out and gently rubbed her back. She simultaneously loathed and loved these moments, when he'd be so tender with her while he knew she was fragile. If she let her guard down and let him comfort her, he'd be inside.

And inside meant he could hurt her.

"What's it like having OCD?" She asked suddenly, turning and looking at him with dull, tired eyes. Demetrius blinked, leaning back a little and considering her question.

"That feels a little out of nowhere. Why do you ask?"

"We've never talked about it. You just… you never talk about it."

"There isn't much to talk about. It's mostly under control at this point."

Bunny flopped backward, laying across the couch on her back, before saying, "Okay, yeah, but I want to know more. I know it's not about, like, cleaning or whatever. But I don't really know anything besides that…" She paused, then shot up again, "Oh my God, that probably makes me a horrible girlfriend. I should have looked into it."

Demetrius laughed, flashing those perfect teeth, as though it was the funniest thing in the world.

"You aren't exactly thoughtful, Bunny. But we all have our weaknesses."

Bunny crossed her arms over her bare breasts. Her lower lip jutted out in a pout while she eyed him.

"Fix that face before I fix that attitude, Bunny," He murmured, and his grin turned playful. She widened her eyes, mouth opening in surprise.

"You're avoiding the question, Demetrius," She snapped, eyes narrowed.

"Alright, fine. Look, it's like this: I constantly have these intrusive thoughts, right? Horrible imagery that goes against everything I believe in. It's triggered by a multitude of things. Doesn't really matter. What does matter is that I've learned how to manage it with medication and therapy."

"What kinds of thoughts?"

"Have you ever seen a puppy and your brain just went, 'Kick it'?"

Bunny shifted uncomfortably before nodding her head.

"Yeah, that happens to everybody. But when you have the type of OCD I have, it's in overdrive. I get those types of thoughts all the time. It's incredibly distressing and can be absolutely paralyzing. The key is that these thoughts aren't wanted, y'know? They're called 'egodystonic,' which means they go against my morals."

She was listening intently, leaning toward him, studying his face as he spoke. As always, his tone was perfectly even, and if there was turbulence beneath the surface, he wasn't betraying a bit of it.

"My dad, he didn't believe in all the mental health stuff at first. It wasn't until I couldn't function and had to be sent home from my boarding school that he took it seriously. I went to a residential treatment center at that point for six months. It was like a boot camp for my brain."

Once he finished speaking, the phone dinged, and they both jumped. After picking it up, Demetrius told her their order was on its way. She crawled over to him, wrapping her arms around his torso and leaning in to bury her face in his neck.

"Can I do anything to help?" She asked meekly.

"You already do more than you know, my love. It's just something I have to live with. It doesn't go away."

"Tell me more."

"Uh, well, the residential place taught

me a lot about how OCD works and how to challenge the intrusive thoughts. Coping mechanisms I can use, that sort of thing. It'll never go away, but I've learned how to live with the thoughts and the severity has lessened. I've put in a lot of hard work to get where I am. It takes a lot to cope through it, but it's worth having my life back in my own hands."

They sat in silence for a few moments before Bunny broke it.

"I love you."

"I love you, too, Bunny."

Chapter 49

Once they'd sopped up all the sauce from their dishes with the crusty slices of Italian bread sent by the restaurant, Bunny and Demetrius lay on the couch tangled in each other's arms again. Her head was on his chest, the coolness of his shirt seeping pleasantly into her skin. He had brought a hand over his stomach to toy with one of her nipples, the peak hardening under his tweaking touch. Bunny whimpered and wriggled, craning her neck so that she could press soft kisses to his neck. Demetrius leaned his head and caught her lips with his, pulling her into a slow, deep kiss that left her breathless.

"I think that's quite enough for today, my love," His words were whispered against her parted mouth, and even though she could smell the olive oil and bread on his breath, she wasn't repulsed.

"Demetrius…" She whined, biting at his jaw. Bunny didn't care about what happened earlier. It was old news. She wanted him now.

"You need to process, Bunny," His tone was deeper now, "What happened earlier was traumatic whether you're willing to face that or not. Besides, we were involved in a scene that lasted an entire day. Your body needs time to recover."

She sat up in a huff, looking away. There was a distant throb between her legs that begged for his tongue, his fingers, his anything. It wasn't fair and, in her mind, it wasn't for him to decide… But she'd let him decide. At the end of the day, their dynamic was built on her trust in his decisions.

A distant ringing broke the silence, and Bunny popped off the couch and padded across the room toward her phone. Demetrius leaned up and watched, curious to see who would be calling her this late. Bunny plucked her phone off of the table and put it to her ear, saying, "Hello?"

In moments, her blood had run cold. She calmly placed the phone back down. She could distantly hear Demetrius asking who it had been, but it felt like someone calling out to her underwater. She turned robotically and walked toward the bedroom. Demetrius followed, voice sounding increasingly frantic as she continued being unresponsive.

Bunny pulled clothing from the dresser in the bedroom, piling it methodically as Demetrius continued to try and get her to talk to him.

"Bunny, please, what's wrong? Bunny?" His voice was high-pitched at this point, betraying his panic as he put his hands on her shoulders and tried to turn her toward him.

She pushed him away without a word, having only shifted marginally, and began dressing. The world felt colder. Something was breaking inside of her that she could hardly name. It was piercing, intense, and unforgiving in its assault.

There was comfort in the simple act of dressing herself; first, the panties, then the bra, and then the pants, and the shirt. Demetrius was breathing hard, staring at her with wide eyes and a gaping mouth.

And then, she did something simply unfathomable to either of them in any other situation: Bunny put her hands to the back of her neck and removed the collar, placing it down on the dresser.

"Bunny, please, just tell me what's wrong, please," His strained voice was overcome.

"I have to go."

"What the fuck are you talking about?"

"Stop."

She tried to push by him, and he stood in her way. Bunny felt the bitter rise of rage creeping up her throat from her burning chest.

"GET THE FUCK OUT OF MY WAY," She roared, shoving him with all the force she could muster.

Demetrius stumbled to the side and she began walking and then began running. He was hot on her heels, calling out in a desperate attempt to reach her, but Bunny could not be reached at this moment.

She shoved her feet into her sneakers. Demetrius stood in the foyer, looking like a heartbroken puppy. Bunny couldn't bring herself to care. Her heart pounded an erratic rhythm in her seizing chest as she grabbed her wallet, ripped open the door, and left without a word.

Chapter 50

It felt like something was crushing her, as though some external force could squeeze her until she shattered into a million pieces like a fragile pane of glass. Even through the pressure, she felt weightless in a dizzying way.

This couldn't be real. It couldn't be. There was so much left unsaid, so many things she wished she could let fall from her mouth in sorrowful, choking waves. Her insides were turning to molten lead.

Her mother was dead.

She was reeling. It couldn't be real, could it? This impossible loss she could feel tearing through flesh and sawing through bone? This woman, who had never protected her, who had only piled onto her suffering, who she would somehow still miss and mourn, was gone.

The crush of sorrow was almost too much to bear. A black hole had opened up inside of her and she was being pulled apart at the seams by the force of it. Fire filled her chest, a fierce burn that made each breath feel like raking coals against her raw throat.

It was getting late. The sun hung low in the sky, crimson bleeding in a cloudy pool across the horizon, and she was pounding beer from a 12-pack she had picked up. From where, she wasn't sure. The last hour of her life had been a smear of tears; the world was blurry in front of her raw, red eyes. She sat on a ledge, legs dangling as she stared aimlessly toward the river rushing below.

The park had cleared out already, a few stragglers still hanging around for likely unsavory reasons she didn't care to consider. When the footfalls sounded behind her, she didn't react. She knew he would find her. He always did, like a cadaver dog put to the scent of a rotting corpse. Bunny felt like she was decaying.

"Bunny, please, you need to come home." His voice was soft, a gentle touch that made her recoil. She said nothing. If she did, the words would be slurred and the moment would be broken. She didn't want to snap back into reality. This was fine, here where she could separate herself from the hurt.

"What? Are you just going to ignore me? I think I deserve more than that, Bunny," He said in a low, desperate tone.

"Go away."

Her voice sloshed in her mouth much like the beer in the can she was trying to guide to her lips.

A hand closed over hers, tightening until she was held in a vice grip that refused to loosen even as she tried to shake it off. Bunny growled, an animalistic sound courtesy of her drunken state. Demetrius simply knelt and wrapped his other hand around her own. He pried her fingers open, throwing the can over the ledge into the river.

"Enough, Bunny. That's enough."

With those words, she collapsed in on herself. Her tears came hot and fast, and Bunny sucked in a deep, desperate breath. Demetrius gathered her into his arms, wrapping a hand around her head and pressing her face into his wool peacoat. It was bitterly cold and she hadn't noticed until just then. Her frost-kissed skin burned as the wool itched against it.

"Bunny, baby, we need to get you inside," He whispered into her hair, hugging her tight.

"It hurts," She managed to gasp out around her panting, snot bubbling as her breath continuously hitched.

"I know, sweetheart, I know." He pulled her up, holding her tight and kissing the top of her head.

She couldn't help but wonder what she had done to deserve this- any of this, the positive or negative. While she bathed in the bliss of knowing this incredible man loved her with everything he had, she felt torn to pieces with the realization that the person who had brought her life had lost her own. Bunny then realized she didn't even know how it happened and screamed into his chest when the force of that thought hit her. Her father had just said she'd "dropped dead" and Bunny had hung up immediately.

She clung to his coat and sobbed.

Chapter 51

The funeral was built on the same humble foundation Bunny hailed from. Demetrius had tried to intervene, insisting he could arrange something more suited to the enormous grief that settled over her like a sopping blanket. Her reaction had been so intense that he hadn't brought the topic up again.

Later, she had apologized, and he had brushed it off. She wasn't herself. He knew that. The mourning had turned her into a monster. Instead, he'd insisted that she schedule an emergency meeting with her therapist and that they increase the number of sessions dramatically.

Drooping bouquets were perched precariously in cracked pots, a second thought thrown next to the woman in the casket as though she were worth nothing to those who put the event together. It was a bitter pill to swallow to realize that this was, in fact, the case.

Bunny wore a simple black dress with her usual band of diamonds marking her as Demetrius'. She had fastened the necklace tighter than usual. Her heels were also black with a modest heel that she walked carefully in to avoid stumbling on her unsteady legs.

The walk toward the open casket was the worst part for her. Until that moment, that terrible moment where she laid eyes upon the too-still woman lying encased in white, she could imagine it wasn't real. It had been a brain aneurysm that had taken her, a detail she'd had to beg from her father when she called him back.

She stood, Demetrius dutifully by her side, his hand resting softly on the small of her back. Her downcast eyes brimmed with tears, red-rimmed from those that had fallen before and still beaded her eyelashes. In the background, she could hear her father, loudly discussing the loss of income from her social security checks.

Bunny leaned down, close to her mother's face, and hissed, "Fuck you. Fuck you for everything. But especially fuck you for dying before I was able to say any of this to you." She rested a kiss on the woman's cheek and then turned on heel with a mission clear in her movement.

Demetrius protested as he realized what she was about to do. She shook him off and walked toward the man who had tormented her for so long. Fury flooded her body, burning brightly as she brought her hand back, and swung it with all the force she could muster. The slap landed with an impossibly loud sound. The small crowd fell silent with a whooshing hush. Her father's face quickly flitted through multiple shades of red. However, he made no move to retaliate.

Instead, he did something so much worse. "You know, Barbara," He began, turning back to face her finally, "She didn't even want you. Wanted to get an abortion. But I convinced her that she'd go to hell. Wasn't too soon after you were born that I realized she'd been right." Bunny froze. The rage had faded into a sickening emptiness. This was it; she was certain it was the end of this part of her life.

"Bunny, please, let's go," Demetrius was

holding her elbow firmly, staring her father down as he did so. She allowed him to lead her away, lost in a haze of emotion she couldn't quite pick apart.

They walked out of the dilapidated church into a frozen world, the sky gray and brooding. It was a fitting scene for the mood set by the previous interaction. Demetrius had let go of her elbow and instead held her still-stinging hand. He continuously gave her reassuring squeezes, glancing over from time to time as they made their way to the car.

As soon as she slid into the passenger seat, she closed the door and leaned her head against the cool glass. Bunny didn't have any tears left to cry. What her father had said didn't cut nearly so much as it might have once upon a time. She had learned her worth. Nothing he said could take that away from her.

"You've grown so much, Bunny," Demetrius said after a few moments of silence, "I'm so proud of you for standing up to him." She couldn't help but smile softly.

Chapter 52

It had been a few weeks since the funeral. Bunny didn't regret not staying for the burial, and she hadn't visited the grave, either. She wasn't sure that she ever would. That part of her life seemed so foreign now, as though it was a different timeline altogether. Therapy had helped and she had continued to attend sessions twice a week at Demetrius' insistence. It was important to him that she take care of her mental health and he made this no secret.

She was lying on the couch in her usual getup; naked with a collar. Demetrius was in his study. She knew he was looking over houses to buy, and she was terrified at the prospect of settling down that way with him. She knew a proposal would come soon after, or perhaps even before the final documents were signed. Bunny wasn't sure she was ready for that, now or ever. There was a certain finality in accepting legal attachment to this man. But haven't I given him everything else? She thought wistfully to herself, reminiscing about the last few months of her life.

One thing was for certain: the question was coming. It would be popped. Bunny needed to be ready for that eventuality and have a game plan for what she would do or say during that dreaded moment. She just couldn't reconcile the fear she felt with the longing to be his entirely.

Bunny flopped onto her side, toying with the fluff of the blanket underneath her. When footsteps sounded in the hall, she looked over her shoulder and saw Michael approaching.

"What do you want, Michael?" She yelped, startled that she hadn't heard the door open.

"Oh, shit, you're naked. Huh. Anyway, where's Demetrius?" He didn't seem phased by her nudity in the least, and she was past the point of caring.

"Too busy for you."

"That I highly doubt, dearest Bunny."

With that, he headed down the hall where the bedrooms were. She had no idea what he wanted, but he had been carrying a rather conspicuous black box. Bunny huffed. She had been hoping that her nakedness would have at the very least made him bashful. Instead, he seemed entirely unphased.

She briefly wondered how often he'd stumbled into the same scene with other conquests of Demetrius' and the thought made her blood boil. It was quelled quickly by the realization that he was no longer on the market, however. The others may have had him first, but she had him forever, and that's what mattered.

But it brought up another realization: she didn't truly have him yet. She wouldn't unless she accepted what she was sure was an upcoming request for her hand in marriage. This brought her back in a perfect circle to the original problem, which was her inability to commit which continued to rear its head with each new phase of their relationship. This next one just felt so final.

Two sets of footsteps could be heard coming down the hallway and Bunny sat up, looking curiously over at the two men who stood at the mouth of the room. Neither seemed to pay her much mind as they chatted a bit about nothing she cared about. In a few moments, they were saying their goodbyes, and Michael was leaving with a quick nod thrown her way.

Bunny stared at Demetrius as he approached, noticing the black box was now in his hands. He kneeled in front of her on the floor and put the box on the couch. She froze.

"Relax, my love. It's nothing you don't want," He said soothingly. At that, she perked up. He opened it and she gasped in delight. Inside were a set of perfectly plump strawberries, all coated in milk chocolate with a white drizzle. Bunny picked one up immediately and began eating it, holding a cupped hand below her chin to catch falling shards of the coating.

"I want to go somewhere special tonight," Demetrius continued, reaching a hand out to stroke her cheek as she continued happily eating her present.

When she looked at him quizzically, he simply smiled, got up, and walked back toward his study.

They were standing in front of the barn. She was suspicious and had been since he'd driven them to this location. Brianna was nowhere to be found. She blew warm air into her hands, which were covered in wool mittens, the same shade of milky white as the thick scarf protecting her neck from the cold.

"Demetrius, it's cold and late," She whined, pouting as he led her into the aisle. By the time they had left the apartment, the sun had long gone down.

"Hush."

It was good-natured and she knew that backtalk would land her in a world of hurt later— literally. So, she bit her tongue and padded along after him. They walked to the end and he swept an arm out toward the empty stall to the left. Or, the stall that was supposed to be empty. Inside stood a tall, handsome chestnut with four white stockings and kind eyes. She looked at him, back at the horse, and then back to him.

Demetrius smiled and said, "He's yours if you like him. My mother found him while in Amsterdam and fell in love. She doesn't have any use for him, so she thought he'd make a lovely gift and a solution to your horse problem."

Bunny opened her mouth to protest and then promptly shut it. She couldn't reject a gift from Katarina. It was unspoken, but likely what the woman considered her Christmas present to Bunny. Tears pricked at her eyes as a mix of emotions swirled to the surface. The kindness his family had shown her was not something she was used to. She was never sure how to react in the face of familial warmth.

"He's lovely," She whispered, opening the stall door and walking in. The smell of shavings and hay was a welcome comfort as she approached the animal. He snorted softly and closed the distance between them, jutting out his face. Bunny lifted a hand and settled it on his nose, looking him over. He was fine-boned, but not in a way that made him conformationally unsound. Instead, it suited his build, and she could tell her would be a beautiful mover.

Demetrius had come in beside her and wrapped his arms around her waist, head resting on her shoulder. "I have one more surprise, my love."

They walked out of the stall and she noticed the shiny tack box that was more than likely now hers. Demetrius motioned for her to open it and she hesitated but bent down to unlatch the top. When she saw the contents, her heart began hammering an unsteady beat. There was a gorgeous collar inside.

It was deep, dark blue with a large white bow at the front that held a large diamond at the center. Gold chains hung in loops, connecting to a ring fastened at the front just underneath the bow. Decorative diamonds dotted the band of the collar, alongside pearls. But that wasn't what gave her pause. In the middle, nestled in a small box, was a ring. It was a simple thing, a small diamond fastened in gold.

"Bunny, I need you to commit to me entirely."

She glanced over her shoulder at him, the paleness of her skin even whiter for the blood that had drained from her face.

"Demetrius, I can't-"

"Yes, you can."

His voice was firm, eyes steady and unblinking. There was a vein of panic in his voice, however, and his gaze was softly pleading. Bunny picked up the collar in one hand and the ring in the other. She stood up slowly, turning to face him, refusing to look at him. Demetrius slid a hand under her chin and forced her to face him.

"Bunny, you're already mine. You always have been. But we need to make it official. It's time to let go of your old life. You don't have to be afraid anymore, my love. You're safe. I promise that I will always protect you and that I will guide you through this to the best of my ability. But I need you to promise your hand to me for my own sake."

He took a shaky breath before continuing. "I know things have been hard since your mother passed, and this might be too soon, but I can't let it wait any longer. I want you to be mine in every way there is. You are everything to me, and I need the world to know that. I need to ensure you are protected and kept safe no matter what happens, and that is only possible if we unify legally. Please, Bunny, let me own you in every way that matters."

They stood there, eyes locked, time seemingly frozen. Bunny felt the coolness of tears rolling down her face and her mouth opened slightly. She wasn't sure what to say. What could she say?

At that moment, something snapped.

"Yes."

Demetrius now looked genuinely shocked, his eyes widening and his body leaning forward as he searched her face for some trace of hesitation.

"What?" He whispered.

"Yes. I'll do it. I'll marry you."

"Are… you serious?"

"   No. I'm fucking with you, Actually, I've been thinking we should break up lately," She said flatly in return, rolling her eyes. Demetrius barked with laughter before picking her up and swinging her around, hooting and hollering the entire time. She shrieked, yelling at him to put her down and stop scaring the horses. Unfortunately for her, there wasn't a reaction to be seen because they were all bombproof.

However, he acquiesced to her demand and settled her feet back on the floor. Demetrius then began kissing the freckles on her face, telling her how much he loved her between each one.

"Can we go home now?" She whined, eyes heavy with fatigue. It hadn't been a particularly grueling day, but the emotions of the moment were beginning to take their toll on her energy levels.

"Of course, baby. Anything you want."

"Okay, in that case, I want to bring him with us and keep him in the living room," She said as she pointed to the horse. Demetrius snorted and rolled his eyes. He then took the ring from her hands and slid it on her finger. It was unceremonious in exactly the way she wanted it to be.

On their way back to the car, he mentioned that they had Christmas dinner with his parents in a few days. Bunny hadn't realized how close they were to the holiday. She had gotten Brianna to agree to come with them, lured by the promise of the best meal she'd ever have.

Bunny realized that, for once, she didn't feel a looming horror at the idea. She was even looking forward to it.

Epilogue

It had been a few months since their wedding. Bunny had demanded a low-key affair with only a handful invited. Demetrius had delivered in full. She could feel a warmth welling in her throat at the sight of the diamond on her ring finger every time her eyes flitted in its direction.

But the ring was nothing compared to the collar. She now sported it proudly as the ultimate symbol of his devotion to her, and her acceptance of it.

Time began to heal her wounds as she put distance between herself and the events that had rocked her so thoroughly just a few months prior. Bunny was still in intensive therapy, and that was unlikely to change anytime soon.

They were sitting on the chaise lounge,

her head in his lap, his hand stroking her hair. "I want to recreate that first chase through the woods," Bunny said. It was one of her fondest memories.

Demetrius chuckled, squeezing her hip. "I think we can make that happen, honey Bunny." She shifted out of his lap, sitting herself up so that she was leaning against one arm, hand braced on his thigh. On a shaky breath, Bunny said, "What if we went all out?"

"What do you mean, baby?"

"I want to do a full CNC scene."

"Are you sure?"

"Yeah, I am."

Even with her firm approval of the idea, she could see a wave of apprehension pass over his face. It likely wasn't that he wouldn't enjoy it, but rather because he wanted Bunny to understand the amount of stress, physical and mental, long scenes could pile on. She wanted him to understand that she did.

"What were you thinking, honey Bunny?" He purred, wrapping an arm around her naked waist and pulling her body into his.

"How about a kidnapping? You chase me through the woods, catch me, and then proceed to ravish me over the next couple of days."

"You've thought this through already, haven't you?" He sounded impressed, albeit amused. The corners of his mouth perked and Bunny leaned forward to kiss one of them.

Demetrius pulled back, humming softly.

"Alright, baby. Let's think on it for a few days then talk it over?"

Bunny's lips curled in a smile, her mind already eagerly plotting out what she wanted. But her true joy was in the knowledge, deep in her bones that it was just one of many adventures to come.

Thank You

FOR READING

About the Author

JUNIPER HARTMANN

Juniper Hartmann is a woman in her early 30s from New England. You can just call her Junie if it suits your fancy!

Over the past decade, Junie has worked extensively in the professional writing space. Her work has been featured across a multitude of websites spanning many niches and industries.

She's finally decided that it's time to write for fun and not just work... But, in true Junie fashion, she's turned fun *into* work.

Junie's Links

SOCIAL & MORE

JuniperHartmann.com

Instagram.com/JuniperHartmann
Tiktok.com/@JuniperHartmann

Author's Note

THOUGHTS ON THE BOOK

It took me forever to get into Bunny's head... but once I was in, I think I got her down pretty well. The thing is that Bunny is not supposed to necessarily be a likable character, especially at first. She's also not reliable as a narrator and tends to miss a lot.

This will become even more apparent in the next book I'm writing, which is *Run, Rabbit, Run* from Demetrius' perspective. It'll clear up a lot, I think, and answer any lingering questions that you might have still.

I had a really fun time writing this entry in the Demetrius and Bunny saga. I hope that you had a good time reading it! It's been a joy to bring these characters to life. I have a lot of love for both of them and who they developed into.

I'm excited to get into the next book... so, I'll leave this here! Have a great rest of your day, and thank you for reading.

Acknowledgements

THE BEST PEOPLE

Numerous people helped make this book a reality. I was cheered on relentlessly by many friends, all of whom hold a special place in my heart.

To Lex, may your heart always be so bright, and may your pillow always be cold on both sides. You have been an absolutely incredible source of encouragement and love.

To Lillith, thank you endlessly for helping me transform the first draft from something barely intelligible to something worth reading.

To my husband, thank you for never giving up on me and cheering me on as I chase my dreams. I could never thank you enough.

A huge shoutout goes out to everybody on my Discord server. You're all incredible (especially my group of "Taylors"!). Whenever I've felt like giving up, you've stood firm in your support, and that has helped keep me going even through the worst of my doubts.

And, of course, to you, the reader. Without you, I wouldn't have a reason to write books at all. Thank you for taking the time to sit down with my book and give it a chance. I am forever grateful to you.

REVIEWER
@10THOUSAND_MEGS

"I have good news and bad news. Bad news first. You're gonna need a freezing cold shower every time you put this book down and have to return to reality. Good news? You'll only have to do that once because The Hare in his Snare ties you down and makes you feel so good you'll beg for more.

Juniper Hartmann spoils us with another eminently readable erotic novel with smoking hot spice, swoonworthy aftercare, and laugh-out-loud moments when we need them most."

Taylor B.

"I absolutely adored getting a more in depth look at Bunny & Demetrius' relationship and how they got started! I loved the every bit of this book. The way Demetrius protected Bunny and helped her through her trauma, pushing her out of her comfort zone and listening to / respecting her boundaries. Demetrius really is the consent KING!

Bunny's trauma really shows through on the page and the way Demetrius is fiercely protective of her makes my heart burst. I could never get enough of these two."

Brittany M.

REVIEWER
@BRIARIEREADS

"I really wasn't sure I could love these characters more than I did when I read Run, Rabbit, Run. I was so wrong!

Seeing their relationship evolve from the beginning was so intense! Demetrius had the best way of making Bunny feel safe, respected, and loved. He balanced her chaos so incredibly well. And the aftercare was EVERYTHING!"

A·R· Nyx

R E V I E W E R
@X_NYXREVIEWS_X

"Wow- I never though Bunny and Demetrius could get better and I was wrong, I loved their story in Run, Rabbit, Run but finally getting the backstory to them was amazing! They are definitely couple goals if you will and their dynamic was incredible!

I was so looking forward to this for weeks and I wasn't disappointed at all. Junie can definitely make your emotions pull with her words and how well she describes everything! This was a 10/10 on all boards for me and I will forever cherish Bunny and Demetrius. I highly recommend this as long as you read trigger warnings before hand, your mental health matters most."

Kelsey C

REVIEWER
@KELI_READS

"Juniper Hartmann has done it again with an amazing book. Putting into words the work that Junie does with her books feels impossible. I was lucky enough to read her debut Run Rabbit Run as an ARC and was blown away. Now having read The Hare in His Snare (the prequel to RRR) made the story line so much better!

Getting to see the beginning of Bunny and Demetrius was perfection. From how they met to their backgrounds to their journey together and everything that led into Run Rabbit Run kept me reading and holding onto every detail from start to finish."

Destiny L.

REVIEWER
@SMUTANDSUCCULENTS

"I was so happy to learn more about Bunny and her backstory, I feel we knew the surface of what made Bunny feel the way she did in RRR, but hearing why absolutely broke my heart.

There were times I was arguing with her about not letting Demetrius buy her things and spoil her and calling her safe word for those moments, and there were times when I was reminded why she was feeling so hesitant toward being spoiled and having that fully security."

www.ingramcontent.com/pod-product-compliance
Lightning Source LLC
Chambersburg PA
CBHW031834310726
48972CB00005B/1277